I0761708

Anywhere With You

Anywhere With You

by

Margo Glynn

2025

ANYWHERE WITH YOU

ISBN 13: 978-1-63679-907-0

This Trade Paperback Original Is Published By
Bold Strokes Books, Inc.
P.O. Box 249
Valley Falls, NY 12185

First Edition: September 2025

THIS IS A WORK OF FICTION. NAMES, CHARACTERS, PLACES, AND INCIDENTS ARE THE PRODUCT OF THE AUTHOR'S IMAGINATION OR ARE USED FICTITIOUSLY. ANY RESEMBLANCE TO ACTUAL PERSONS, LIVING OR DEAD, BUSINESS ESTABLISHMENTS, EVENTS, OR LOCALES IS ENTIRELY COINCIDENTAL.

Credits
Editor: Ruth Sternglantz
Production Design: Stacia Seaman
Cover Design by Inkspiral Design

Anywhere With You

CHAPTER ONE

I watched on my phone as Bridget enjoyed a sloppy, open-mouthed kiss with her childhood best friend, then kept watching as the reel started over again. I didn't gag, like I had the first time. No, by my twentieth viewing, I only sat and stared.

"Honey," Florence said.

It wasn't an endearment. That's my name, unfortunately.

"Oh, Honey," she said again, and this time I wasn't sure. "She's not worth your tears."

I'd like to state for the record that I was not crying. I was, in fact, watching with perfectly dry eyes as my wife kissed a man who had spoken, no, not just spoken, *orated* on his love for *his* own wife in my own backyard six months ago.

One kiss, two marriages, and three hundred thousand dollars sunk into a business that I would now have to get a lawyer and fight to keep. And would still probably lose.

But for now, I slid my phone into my pocket and put on a grin that made Florence cringe. "Is there anything you need, Florence?" My voice was too high normally. At the moment, I sounded like a songbird being plucked.

She gave a sympathetic head tilt. Florence couldn't be older than fifty, but she'd been raised by—and possibly possessed by the spirit of—an elderly aunt from the Deep South. "I was going to ask if you're ready for me to go to lunch, but if you're feeling poorly—"

"No!" I almost shouted. "I mean…no, not at all. Go ahead."

I rushed Florence out of the store and took her spot at the front of the shop.

Strings & Things had been my dream, not my wife's. Sure,

Bridget knew enough to help beginners find a violin, but those sales were rare. It was the electric guitars in the front window that brought in customers. It was the row of acoustics, from cheap to elite, that brought in the sales. It was my passion, in short, that made this a business and not a very expensive display case.

And now…well, now there was a very thin pile of receipts and a very thick manila envelope on my desk. The thin pile of receipts represented our week's sales. The thick, unopened manila envelope was from a law firm. It was addressed to me, and only me.

It had arrived this morning, when I was half awake and wondering who was rude enough to ring a doorbell at seven a.m. A man in a suit had confirmed my name and placed it in my hands. If he said anything after that, I didn't hear, and I may not have answered him. I closed the door and went back to bed.

I hadn't wanted to leave it there, haunting my house while I was at work, so I brought it with me. Now, I shoved it under the receipts and opened Bridget's Mesmio page instead, watching her French kiss Lorenzo until the entire thing seemed absurd, like when you say the same word again and again until it loses meaning.

Who invented kissing? Why do we push our faces into each other's like that? Why does a declaration of love have to be followed by trading all our mouth bacteria?

I took my phone back out of my pocket and searched *mouth germs under a microscope*.

But just as I hit enter, the bell over the front door tinkled.

There was a long list of people I wasn't eager to see, and Cara Espinoza was number three.

Her short black curls were windblown. She wasn't currently crying, but her eyes were red and swollen, which was particularly obvious because Cara had these massive, beautiful eyes. I supposed they were brown, technically, but that was like saying the ocean was blue. It didn't come close to expressing all the hues and depth.

As if that wasn't enough, she had lips like Selena. Bridget and I had actually had conversations about her lips. We thought we could probably get her some red lipstick and eyeliner and teach her to sing "Bidi Bidi Bom Bom." She'd be internet-famous overnight.

For comparison, Bridget and I agreed that I looked like the musician Norah Jones, who coincidentally is also the daughter of an

Indian father and white Texan mother, but a version of Norah that is washed out, short, just shy of forty years old, and thirty pounds heavier. Only my long, thick brown hair and side-swept purple bangs improved the situation.

But Cara Espinoza was not the type to dress up and dance on Mesmio. I doubted she'd ever been to a concert at all. She probably spent Friday nights sipping tea and writing down the license plates of people who drove too fast through her apartment complex. She probably thought cleaning the baseboards and reorganizing her shoes made for exciting weekend plans.

Now, she glanced around at the guitars, the drum sets, the violins and cellos, and the absence of even a single customer, before her eyes landed on me.

"Did you know, Honey?" she rasped.

I recognized that rasp. I'd been the embodiment of that rasp for weeks, but somehow, that didn't make me sympathize with her. Instead, rage blazed up in me in an instant like a fire that hadn't quite been smothered. My words felt mean before I even spoke them, but I had been teetering for weeks between being okay and losing my shit completely.

Cara was just the last straw, the one that tipped the balance, the butterfly that landed on the wrong damn seesaw.

"Did I *know*?" I seethed. "Did I *know* that my wife was fucking your husband, Cara? Is that what you're asking me?"

Cara's tears were as close to the surface as my anger. She sobbed once.

She waited, giving me the chance to yell at her more if I wanted, or maybe to apologize.

I did neither. I stared at her until she turned around, the bell over the door tinkling softly again as she fled.

I put my head on the cool countertop next to the cash register and tried to breathe calmly. Honestly, I tried to breathe *at all*.

I was an ass. Obviously.

Cara, sweet Cara, did not deserve to be screamed at, not by me, not when her worst mistake was the same as mine: She'd loved the wrong person.

Chapter Two

Florence came back from lunch, proclaiming that it was "Hotter'n the devil's armpits out there."

She took her spot at the register with another frustratingly pitying smile at me, and I retreated to my office, pushed aside the paltry stack of receipts, and picked up the envelope from the lawyers.

Honoria Singh, it said in the center. The font was gigantic. What was that, 20 point?

I wondered why they didn't just mail it. It wasn't like they had a therapist bring it to make sure the recipient could handle the emotional hailstorm that followed. No, they had a man in a suit do it instead of a nice, friendly postal worker.

I was always forgetting to stop by the mailbox. Bridget had always been the mail checker, but then again, she was always the one who had ordered something and was waiting for it to arrive: earrings, coffee mugs, clothes that probably wouldn't fit. I didn't think she even wanted most of that crap. She just liked to get packages. She never even tracked the deliveries, just waited to be surprised.

She'd left so much behind when she moved out that I felt she'd proved my point.

Now, there was an envelope for me, one that I hadn't asked for and was certain not to want.

I turned it over and over in my hands.

I was delaying. I literally lifted the envelope to my nose and sniffed it just so I could do something other than open it.

I put it down.

I picked it back up again.

I couldn't open it. I couldn't start that next part of my life yet, not when this one had, until recently, been so damned good.

My phone vibrated in my pocket. It said *Dad* and had a picture of him about to take a massive bite of an ice cream cone, mouth stretched comically wide.

I could ignore the call, but he would likely just keep calling because he was retired and didn't have any hobbies.

"Hello?"

"Your mother is trying to poison me," he said, then swore in Telugu. Dad had moved to Houston from Hyderabad when he was nineteen, alone. He'd never gone back, though he still talked about it from time to time.

Since the creation of video chat, he had become much closer to our family in India, and I'd met aunts and uncles and grandparents virtually that I'd only known from the occasional letter and awkward phone call.

"What?" I said with elaborate shock. "Did Mom try to sneak vegetables into your food again?"

"She made sweet potato brownies, Honey. It's a travesty. She should be locked up."

"I'll call the FBI, right now."

"Call the UN. These sweet potatoes are Canadian."

I laughed, then realized I was still holding the horrid envelope and put it down, then pushed it to the far side of my desk so I couldn't accidentally pick it up again. "How are you, Dad?"

"Not too bad, not too bad. I'm generally a cheery guy, don't you know? How are you doing, my Honey?"

Before I could come up with a believable lie, my mother picked up the other extension.

Yes, they were calling on an honest-to-God landline, maybe one of the last in existence.

"Honoria!" my mother exclaimed, and I made the audible gagging sound I always made when she used my full name. She was never deterred.

To be fair, nothing had ever been able to deter my mother. She played the trombone in college—I suspect because someone once told her she was too petite for it. Throughout my childhood, she had brought it out to play the happy birthday song and Christmas carols, or to blast in my direction when I overslept as a teenager.

My father had played the trumpet back then. He'd never touched it after graduation.

That was how they'd met, in the college band, being loud together.

Growing up, I swore I'd never touch a brass instrument, but the music bug had bitten me anyway. I played guitar, bass, drums, piano, and ukulele. I'd even learned a bit of the trombone once I was an adult, but I'd never tell Mom about it.

"How's sweet little Badger?" she asked.

"Badger is fine," I replied, glancing at his photo on my office bookshelf. He was a tiny black mop of a mutt, not the Labrador or Great Dane that I always imagined I'd have. Instead, I had a miniature gremlin, a purse dog if ever there was one, and Bridget had said she loved him, then had walked out on him as effortlessly as she'd walked out on me. "He loves his new doggy door. Zooms in and out of the backyard all day long. I'm fine, too, by the way. Thanks for asking about my *dog* first, Mother."

"Mm. How are you really?" Mom asked. She obviously didn't know about the envelope on my desk, but she knew that Bridget had moved out, leaving both me and Badger behind. Mom found both abandonments incomprehensible. I hadn't told her about the Mesmio reels. She would've seen them as an added betrayal.

And she would've been right.

I sighed. "I feel like I've barely survived a hurricane. My home, my store, and my future are suddenly entirely uncertain. But I'm at work today, so good for me." I cringed. I was not good at lying.

Unlike my wife, who was apparently awesome at it.

"Good," Dad said at the same time Mom said, "Are you sure that's wise?"

Dad went on. "You know that if you need anything, we are here for you."

"You can even have your old room back," Mom said. My eyes found the picture next to Badger, one that had sat on my bedside table in that old room. Teenaged me was making a *wow* face, standing next to the poet Mary Oliver, who was signing a book for me. I loved that picture and that book.

Now my bedside table held a picture of Bridget and me on our wedding day. I wore a deep purple A-line dress with a sweetheart neckline and shimmery silver along the hem. Bridget wore a full ball gown in blush pink. I had to wade through tulle to kiss her. She'd been incredibly beautiful, shining with happiness, unwilling to let go of my hand even to let me pass my bouquet to my maid of honor.

"Honey?" Mom asked. "Are you listening?"

"Yes. Sorry. What did you say?"

"You can have your old room back. Anytime you want. I can—"

"No, thank you. Ever. No matter how many times you offer," I said. Honestly, I'd lost count. "And now I'd like to talk about literally anything else. How's the garden, Mom?"

Dad gave an exaggerated sigh of annoyance, but she immediately started telling me about how many types of tomato plants she'd planted and that she'd learned about companion planting them with basil and marigolds and that she got up at dawn every morning to search the leaves for hornworms because you could blink and they'd have eaten every leaf on the whole plant. You'd go out and have nothing but naked stems.

She talked, and I listened with every bit of my focus because her brain seemed like a happier place to be than mine was at the moment.

When she was finished, Dad started telling me about a really good steak he'd eaten, in detail.

"Where was this?" I asked.

"At home. I cooked it," Mom said.

"That's ninety percent of the reason I married her," Dad said.

"I won't ask about the other ten percent," I said, and they both giggled. Actually giggled.

I grew up with this. My whole life, it's been the two of them, arguing and laughing and making comments about each other that I finally got old enough to understand and immediately wished I hadn't. It was disgusting. It was annoying.

And it was no wonder I grew up believing in love.

CHAPTER THREE

Florence agreed to open for me the next day, so instead of heading to work Saturday morning, I kissed Badger's overexcitable little head and went to apologize to Cara Espinoza.

I'd always liked her and Lorenzo's apartment. The building was surrounded by young trees and flowerpots, and there were always chalk drawings in bright pink and yellow on the sidewalks.

Cara and Lorenzo didn't have kids, and neither did we. Thank goodness no children would suffer from Bridget and Lorenzo's betrayal. The two of them could go drive off a cliff or get eaten by alligators, and who would care? No one.

I knocked hesitantly on Cara's door, and she opened in seconds. I'd been worried it was too early for a weekend, but she was already dressed in a green T-shirt and jeans with lace at the hem, her hair fixed in its big, beautiful curls, and the faint bit of makeup she wore was already applied. She really was very pretty, in an uptight schoolteacher kind of way.

I was wearing a black tank top and pants that I'd bought based on their claims to *minimize stomach bulge*, which is exactly the phrase that every woman wants to read when shopping. I honestly didn't worry too much about stomach bulge, in general. I considered that having a body was an eighty-ish year privilege, if I was lucky, and that if I could spend that time focusing on my awesome guitar calluses and my elbow-length hair, and *not* my stomach bulge, I'd be much happier.

I tried to stop thinking about stomach bulges because Cara was standing there, waiting for me to speak.

I smiled. She cringed at my smile.

That was happening a lot lately. I really needed to look in a mirror.

"I'm sorry," I said immediately. One of Dad's favorite life lessons was to apologize as often as you can, to practice until you're good at it.

I did much better with that advice than with his other lessons, which were some nonsense about oil changes and filing my taxes early.

Cara was still standing there, not saying anything.

"I brought pastries," I said.

She eyed the bag. "Mademoiselle Louise Bakery?"

I nodded. I didn't know Cara's opinion, but I would forgive Darth Vader for a Mademoiselle Louise croissant.

Apparently, Cara agreed. She opened the door wide, and I went inside.

Cara's apartment was immaculate. It could've been in a TV show about people who have their shit together.

Bridget and I usually hosted dinners in our backyard, but we had visited Cara and Lorenzo before. I always assumed that they made a special effort to clean up before they had guests. I couldn't have imagined that they lived this way.

I wasn't a slob, and Bridget was almost not a slob, but our house had nice, uneven stacks of books and coasters on the tables, junk mail on the counter, the occasional sock between the couch cushions, and floors littered with dog toys.

Cara had clean surfaces, straight throw pillows, and no dishes—not a *single dish*—in the sink. Even the spot under the stovetop burners that is perpetually filthy in every house I'd ever visited was shining, pristine. If I didn't know better, I'd swear that no one had ever actually lived here.

I followed Cara to the kitchen table, because of course we wouldn't be shoving pastries into our mouths on the living room couch like commoners, and she told me to have a seat while she grabbed plates.

"Coffee?" she said, gesturing to the already full coffeepot.

"Yes, please."

She poured the coffee in a porcelain cup and brought creamer in a tiny porcelain pitcher and a matching sugar bowl.

"Dear God, do you always live this way?" I couldn't help it, but the regret hit me instantly. I had come here to apologize to this woman, not to criticize the way she served coffee.

But she didn't seem offended. "Didn't you ever play with fancy tea sets as a kid and think, one day I'll grow up and have the real thing?"

"No."

She rolled her eyes and brought over two small plates for our pastries, then sat across from me with her own cup. "Well, I did. And now I have teapots, and cups that don't advertise John Deere tractors, and really, really good bath towels."

I had my mouth open for a rebuttal but stopped at that last one. Really, really good bath towels. I'd always meant to buy some. That was a luxury, but a luxury I could probably afford. Maybe they wouldn't fundamentally enhance my quality of life, nothing that extreme. But they would improve my enjoyment of it.

Maybe that was her point.

"You're really smart," I said.

She snorted, then reached for the pastries. "Maybe. But my husband had been cheating for six months, so I may not be smart about some things."

A cold feeling crept into my stomach. "Six months?" I breathed.

Cara's head jerked up to look at me. She didn't say a word.

I pulled in a shaky breath. "I didn't know it had been that long. I didn't think to ask."

Cara took a pastry, placed it in the center of her plate, and passed the bag to me. I took the one that looked like it contained the most calories and bit into it, hoping that the sugar and the fat and all the bad stuff would momentarily make me feel better. I chewed and swallowed and drank my coffee, not tasting any of it.

"When did he tell you he was leaving?" I asked, and I instantly regretted that, too. What was the point of knowing? Was I hoping to compare the length of Cara's suffering to mine? I took another large bite.

Cara sighed but answered at once, as though she wanted to talk about it, maybe as though she didn't have two parents and a coworker who were constantly pestering her to talk through her emotions.

"It's been six weeks or so," she said. "He said Bridget was doing the same, that same day. I kept thinking that I'd call you or go by, but it wasn't until yesterday…" She stopped, took a sip of coffee, then cleared her throat and met my eyes. "Yesterday, he called to check on me."

I cringed and didn't try to hide it. "Did you tell him to fuck off?"

Cara's eyes widened, and something about her changed, became more open, like the edges of her mask were slipping. "No," she said, and it was almost a whine. "Why didn't I tell him to fuck off? Honey, what's wrong with me? Can I call him right now and tell him to fuck off?"

I almost laughed. I probably would've, but there was a manic edge to Cara. I was a little afraid that the wrong reaction would make her start crying or throwing things.

"You can, if you want," I said. "But for maximum impact, I'd wait until he calls again."

"Right. Good thinking. Anyway, he's been cheating on me since Thanksgiving." She gave another wide, fake smile, then shook her head. "Maybe he was calling because he really did want to know if I was okay. I don't know. I'm not sure I care."

Thanksgiving. This was March.

Maybe I should call Bridget. I could ask her if she looked at our wedding picture every day or if she was, instead, not a pathetic mess of emotion. I could check on her. Or I could just tell her to fuck off, too.

"Bridget did tell you that day, didn't she? Right after Valentine's Day?" Cara asked.

I nodded. "Right after Valentine's Day, but not close enough after so that I could get a bunch of Valentine's-themed breakup grief candy half off."

Cara said she'd thought about calling me, but I'd never considered calling her. I'd spent every waking hour in Strings & Things so I didn't have to be at home, and I cycled through all of Bridget's social media hourly, at least, because God forbid I missed a detail of her romantic new life.

But no, Cara had never even crossed my mind.

She'd driven across Houston to see me, and I hadn't even picked up the phone.

"I think there are divorce papers on my desk," I said, surprising myself. I hadn't told anyone yet.

"What do you mean you *think*?"

"I haven't opened the envelope."

Cara shook her head. "I opened mine as soon as they came, standing there in the doorway in front of the process server man or whoever. I had just gotten home, and I had my hands full of bills and junk mail and my keys. I tried to pick it all up after, but I know some of it blew away. I guess they'll send new bills, won't they? It's not like I missed my only chance with the electric company."

"I'm sorry," I said because there was nothing else to say. Maybe I meant *I'm sorry you're going through all this*. Maybe, *I'm sorry our spouses are fucking each other*. Maybe, *I'm sorry that I didn't call you when I should have*.

Maybe all of it.

"I'm sorry, too," she said.

[illegible] the [illegible].

[illegible] standing there in the doorway in front of [illegible] had [illegible] my name [illegible] was [illegible] they'd [illegible] the electric company."

[illegible] anything else [illegible] I [illegible] Maybe I [illegible] Maybe [illegible]

[illegible]

[illegible]

Chapter Four

I worked all weekend, which mostly meant sitting in my office watching Mesmio reels of buff women splitting logs.

Florence and our other employee, Doug, were more than capable of running Strings & Things without my constant presence, but the alternative was to be at my house, and Badger's fuzzy face aside, I hated it there. I fantasized a lot about setting it on fire. Not for the insurance. To be honest, I wasn't even sure there was insurance. No, I just wanted to watch it burn…and all the memories with it.

It was nice of Lorenzo and Bridget to both move out, I supposed, leaving Cara and me each with our homes. Or maybe they just didn't want us to know where to find them. As angry as I'd been these last six weeks, that was probably smart.

Not that I'd burn down *their* love nest. But I'd probably spend a lot of time sitting across the street and thinking about it. Or about buying a bag of crickets from the pet store and leaving it outside their bedroom window. Smearing their cars with canned tuna. Getting a Realtor to put their house on the market. Reporting them to the police for smuggling illegal cheeses.

Definitely better not to know.

On Sunday, Bridget and Lorenzo posted another Mesmio reel, kissing on a pier in Galveston, seagulls shrieking alarmingly close by, as though mistaking her phone for food.

Bridget looked like she'd been out in the sun a lot. Her face was tanned, her hair gold streaked. She had a new tattoo on her wrist, some kind of butterfly.

Lorenzo looked like Johnny Depp, if Johnny Depp had been beaten up too many times, but that was how Lorenzo always looked.

I was pretty sure that Bridget was walking along that pier now, gleefully telling Lorenzo that their latest video had been watched seventy-six times. She had no way of knowing that seventy of those views were mine.

I still expected her to call every day. After Cara said that Lorenzo had called, I was sure that I had one coming, too. I spent all weekend with the phone on my desk in front of me, ringer on. I even called from the store phone to check the volume. The horrible default ringtone annoyed Florence, Doug, our one customer, and me. My phone was working fine.

But Bridget hadn't spoken to me since the day she moved out. She hadn't even called to ask about our dog. Not once. I couldn't imagine that degree of heartlessness.

Sunday evening, I set up an amp in the store. We hadn't had any customers in a while, and Doug was deep in the latest Elizabeth Acevedo novel. I sent him to the break room to keep reading so I didn't interrupt. It was a really good book.

I played through my favorites—Eric Clapton's "Layla," some Nirvana and The Kinks.

My mother always insisted that I must want to perform onstage, write my own songs, be a rock star. It was funny because she loved the trombone and never wanted to play onstage either, but she thought it had to be different if the guitar was your instrument.

I was never the most self-aware kid, but I had known this about myself: I wanted to play, not perform.

And I wanted to talk to other people who loved to play. That was how the idea for the shop began. I tried giving lessons as a side gig. I tried writing for music sites. But one day, I went into Guitar Center, one of those big, chain music stores, and I thought *yes*. I can do this, and do it much, much better.

I was halfway through my own version of "Jolene" when the door opened.

I had the amp turned up too high to hear the bell, but I saw the door out of the corner of my eye and stopped playing.

My last chord reverberated, and Cara stopped just in front of me in a tight beige dress, her head held high.

"I have an idea," she said.

Chapter Five

"You want to go on a road trip to make our exes jealous?" I asked twenty minutes later, making sure I'd understood her plan.

We sat on stools near the rows of guitar cases. They were mostly black, but Cara found a bright blue one and absently ran her fingers against the rough plastic. Her nails were short with a beige polish that matched her dress. I kept mine short for playing guitar, and I had a sudden urge to ask why she did the same. Grading papers? Frog dissections?

Cara's cheeks were red, but she didn't seem embarrassed by my words. "No," she said firmly. "I want to get out of town and have an adventure because we deserve it. I want to post reels on Mesmio along the way so that they—and everyone else—know we're even happier now that they're gone."

I looked at her blankly for a moment, wondering if she believed any of that. I had a framed picture of my wedding day on my bedside table that had been held so much that the glass had grown semi-opaque with my fingerprints.

"So, we're not pretending to date or anything?" I asked. "Because I've seen that movie. I know how it ends."

"No," she said again. She had a way of sounding like her calmness took considerable effort. It made me want to keep trying her patience. I wondered if her students ever felt the same. "We're friends," she explained. "We're not pretending anything."

"No offense," I said, running my fingers down the guitar strings, "but we're barely friends. Bridget and Lorenzo were childhood buddies. We're the tagalong spouses. Or we were."

Cara didn't flinch, and for a moment, I wondered if I'd underestimated her. I'd seen her as frail, bulldozed by her husband's infidelity, and that was based on what? The fact that I'd seen her crying? Had toxic masculinity somehow so infested my female brain that I judged someone for publicly expressing an emotion?

I vowed to do better.

"So now's our chance to change that," Cara said. "Think of it as a chance to become better friends. Think of it as a vacation that you don't have to take alone. To be honest, I don't care about your motivations. I just…"

She stopped, looking at the white lilies embroidered along the hem of her dress, and I did think about it.

I thought about getting away from my house, full of memories, from the dread of running into Bridget or Lorenzo at the grocery store, and most of all, from the unopened envelope on my desk.

I thought about my parents' nagging concern, my mother's insistence that I can move back into my childhood bedroom whenever I needed, and Florence's continual declarations of pity.

And I thought about those damned Mesmio reels of Bridget and Lorenzo kissing on the beach, and how I hadn't shared or posted anything on any social media site since Bridget left, and how she probably thought that I was grieving, wallowing in despair, working constantly to manage the pain.

Well, screw her.

"I just think—" Cara said.

"Okay," I interrupted. "I'm in."

Cara looked up, wide-eyed. "Really?"

"Yes. When do we leave?" Suddenly, it sounded like such a good idea that I was ready to race home and pack. Who needs a plan?

"Okay," Cara said, her eyes excited. "Friday is an early release day, and after that is spring break."

"So, Friday?" I asked.

She nodded. "We can take my car. I get excellent gas mileage."

"Yeah, sure, but *where* are we going?"

Cara froze, as though the thought hadn't occurred to her. I, on the other hand, had a thousand ideas, but just then, Doug emerged from the break room, looking cheerful and holding up the book.

"That was so awesome. Thanks, boss."

"Yeah," I said. "Hey, Doug, do you have a favorite vacation spot?"

"Sure. Barbados."

"That's a little out of our price range," I said. "In the contiguous US?"

Doug thought about it, tapping Elizabeth Acevedo against the cash register. "It's a tie. I really love DC. It's fascinating, and you can't beat the Smithsonian. But the redwoods on the West Coast are also unforgettable. And with climate change, who knows how long we'll have them?"

Cara made a small sound of distress. I looked at her, and she seemed to struggle to keep her expression neutral.

"Redwoods, then?" I asked her.

She nodded, and as though she couldn't hold it in for another minute, she smiled hugely, her eyes crinkling.

I turned back to Doug. "Interested in picking up some extra hours next week?"

Doug's grin widened, too. "Always."

Florence's answer, the next morning, was slightly more colorful.

"Well," she said, "I'm happier than a dog with two dicks."

"You're…what now?"

"I'm delighted. I'm so very glad that you're getting out of town and getting some fresh air. You need it. And," she added, unknowingly echoing Cara, "you deserve it."

You can't argue with logic like that.

Chapter Six

If there was any doubt in my mind about my decision, it ended on Monday morning, when Bridget posted a Mesmio reel from the last-minute cruise to Mexico that Lorenzo had bought tickets for.

I watched it four more times, growing a little more irritated each time. Was that why I kept watching her reels? Because feeling grossed out by their spit swapping and annoyed at her flamboyant happiness felt better than sitting alone, heartbroken?

That probably wasn't healthy.

I was a little tempted to ask Cara if Lorenzo had ever bought *her* cruise tickets, not to be an ass but because I was genuinely curious. I'd surprised Bridget with tickets to a concert in Austin, once, and her response had been to complain about the drive and my ruining her weekend plans to take naps and watch reruns of *The Jerry Springer Show*, which was interesting as a time capsule of nineties fashion and as an argument against the continuation of our species, but not for any other reason.

I didn't mention the cruise to Cara. I did call and talk to her about how to split the expenses, what landmarks we didn't want to miss, and—most importantly—who would be in charge of the music.

"I'm obviously more qualified," I argued.

"It's a question of taste, and I'm not a fan of Led Zeppelin."

It took me a moment to even guess at why she thought I was into Led Zeppelin. "Is that what you thought I was playing in the store?"

"Sounded like it."

"It was Dolly Parton."

"It definitely wasn't. What do you think of Iron and Wine?" she asked.

"No," I said. "White Stripes?"

"No. The Decemberists?"

"Franz Ferdinand?"

"The guy whose assassination started World War I?"

"No." I sighed. "Okay, um…Taylor Swift?"

There was a long pause. "Do you actually like Taylor Swift, or are you just giving in?" Cara asked.

"Of course I like Taylor Swift. Everyone likes Taylor Swift."

"Huh," she said. "Who else does everyone like?"

"Pharrell Williams? Lizzo? Adele?"

"Okay, you can be in charge of music. No ABBA."

I gasped. "What do you have against ABBA? No, don't answer that. Save it for the road trip. We'll need conversation topics."

"I'll be in charge of that," Cara offered. "I'll make a list. It's funny. As much time as we've spent together, I don't feel like I know you as well as I should."

Neither of us said why, but I imagined she knew as well as I did—there had been dozens of dinners over the years, but Bridget and Lorenzo had dominated them. They had chosen the days, the menu, the conversations. It wasn't as though Cara and I had sat there in silence, but we certainly hadn't been the main attraction.

For the thousandth time, I thought: I should've seen it coming. I should've known.

"Oh," Cara said. "Don't forget Beyoncé."

"I could never forget Beyoncé. I saw her once at Ragin' Cajun."

Cara gasped. "I knew she was from Houston, but I've never seen her. Did you freak out?"

"Only on the inside. I…" I was about to tell her that I'd had to hold Bridget down to keep her from going to Beyoncé's table, but that memory was tainted now.

Cara seemed to understand. She had her own tainted memories. "Well, I'm officially jealous. Oh! Add Olivia Rodrigo."

"Got it. Text me when you think of anyone else."

"Text me if you find another place you want to stop. I think we have a pretty good list so far."

I nodded, even though I knew she couldn't see me. "I'm actually looking forward to this."

I expected her to laugh and say *of course*, but she didn't. There was a long pause. Then she said, "I am, too. It's the first thing in weeks."

"Getting away will be good. Even though…" I took a breath, hoping she would ignore me. If she hadn't seen the Mesmio reel, I didn't want to be the one to tell her.

"Even though they're on their way to Cozumel," she finished with a sigh.

"Yeah."

"Screwing their way through the Caribbean."

"Yeah."

"Can I just say," she said, "they both really suck."

"Yeah, you can definitely say that."

There was a pause, then the sound of thumping, as though Cara was punching one of her throw pillows.

"Okay," she said, returning to the phone a little breathless. "Now, let's talk about snacks. We'll need chewy options to stay awake while driving, so jelly beans, taffy, maybe some dried fruit? And popcorn. I've got the popcorn covered. I buy it in bulk."

I talked to Cara about snacks, but my mind was on the price. I knew hotels were expensive, and though the state park fees and other attractions we'd chosen were on the cheaper side for vacation destinations, we had the cost of eating every meal on the road, too. One day of restaurants would easily outstrip what I usually spent on groceries in a week.

Bridget had been making enough money for both of us, for so many years, that I'd kind of gotten out of the habit of thinking about daily expenses. It was an incredibly privileged position to be in, I knew.

But now I was splitting the cost of a spring break trip, and I needed to take a serious look at my bank account.

When Cara and I got off the phone, I opened the bank app with my breath held.

When it loaded, I relaxed. Not as bad as I'd feared. It helped that I hadn't gone anywhere or done anything for fun in months. If I postponed paying the house's electric bill and my car insurance, I'd be in excellent shape for the trip.

I wouldn't be at home anyway, I reasoned, and neither would

Badger, so it didn't matter if the electric company got a little fussy, and my car would be parked for the week, too. We were taking Cara's.

The most important thing was that the store was still afloat. My employees and my vendors were all paid.

For now.

What I would keep or lose in the divorce…I couldn't make myself think about it. Not yet. This year had already been too hard. I couldn't conceive of losing anything else.

Chapter Seven

Friday at five a.m., my phone vibrated with a text.

I fumbled my phone off the nightstand and had to hang half my body off the bed to see the screen.

The text said, *Alicia Keys*.

I smiled. I fell back asleep without looking at the wedding picture on my bedside table. But I was thinking about it. I seemed to always be thinking about it.

Four hours later, I was awake and caffeinated. I stopped by the shop to give Florence and Doug last-minute instructions that they did not need. Florence hugged me, and I patted her back.

What would happen if I couldn't keep the store afloat? Now, without Bridget's salary as a life preserver, I could already feel myself sinking, and it was terrifying to imagine pulling Florence and Doug down with me.

But I tried to shake it off as I left. I couldn't solve it all today, and today was the last day I would think about it. I was going on vacation.

I picked up ice for the back-seat cooler full of drinks because according to Cara, "Convenience stores are the biggest scam ever."

I argued that they were, instead, *convenient* but was ignored.

Another text came through: *Florence and the Machine*.

I texted back, *I'm impressed. Now, get back to work. What are your students doing while you're texting?*

Oh, they're texting, too. Nobody smiles as much at their own crotch as a teenager hiding a phone in class. I hope.

I laughed so hard that strangers at the supermarket stared at me.

I went home again long enough to pick up Badger, who was always hesitant about a ride in the car, but willing to go if it meant he didn't get left behind. I didn't tell him about the trip, only that he was going to see his *other* favorite people.

Before we got to the end of the block, he'd jumped all over me and the dash, then got his head stuck between the middle console and the passenger seat. He yipped pathetically until I stopped the car to free him. Then I turned the car around and went back home to get his carrier.

Mom met me at the front door with several packages of homemade monster cookies, putting them into my hands and going to take Badger out of the carrier. Dad came out and scratched Badger's head, then unloaded the bags of toys and food, the leash, the name and phone number for Badger's vet, and twenty other things I was sure he absolutely needed.

Badger wiggled in my mother's grip like his lifelong dream had just come true.

"Traitor," I said. He looked at me with his uneven face and yipped.

"I know you've been through a lot, Honey, but I can't see that running away is a good choice," Dad said, herding us toward the house with his arms full.

"And with…*her*?" Mom said. "Aren't you worried that you're just going to be in an echo chamber of anger the whole time? You need a healing environment. Why don't you just tell her you've changed your mind and come relax here with us for a few days?"

"I'll be fine. Cara and I aren't wallowing anymore. It's been almost two months. We've both been through the five stages of grief, or whatever. Is it only five? It seems like it should be more. And one of them should definitely be vacuuming. That would be handy."

"Just a few days," Mom wheedled. "A week at most. I'll cook whatever you want."

"That's very much not going to happen," I said, "but I appreciate your concern. Actually, that's a lie. I don't. But I do love you both, and I'll take lots of pictures."

They looked at me and sighed simultaneously, which made all three of us laugh.

Mom made me come in and have a cup of coffee before I left. It had never in my life bothered me to scoop sugar out of a Tupperware container, but today it occurred to me that Mom would adore a little sugar bowl and pitcher like Cara's. And she had a birthday coming up.

"Where are you planning on sleeping?" Dad asked.

"Underpasses, park benches, the usual."

Dad stared at me, waiting for a serious answer.

"Well, we realized that we're not backpacking college students. We're adults, so we're going to stay in semi-nice hotels. But we're also broke adults, so we're sharing a room. We actually found a little cabin to rent once we get there, so we'll wake up to the redwoods."

"Oh," Mom said a little wistfully.

"Want to come along?" I asked, grinning. I knew she'd say no, but I also knew that Mom had always loved traveling. In between college and my birth, she and Dad had been to three continents and over a dozen countries.

After that, money got tight. In part it was the expense of a difficult pregnancy and delivery, plus a year of unemployment after Dad was laid off when I was eight, plus my grandfather's long illness, plus house repairs when the pipes—designed for Houston weather and not real winters—burst during a freak ice storm that lasted days and left most of the city without power, plus saving to help me pay for college, and to top it off, an economic system designed to make sure that we all struggle as much as we can until we're dead.

"I wish I could go," Mom said. "But it's planting season, and there's just too much to do here. God knows what the garden would look like if I left for a week. Everything would be dead."

Dad took her hand. "We've never seen the redwoods. What about in the fall? We won't drive. It takes too long. We'll fly."

She smiled at him. "It's a date."

They kissed.

"Ugh, you guys are the worst," I said and stood to leave.

"Honey," Dad said, his voice cajoling me not to run off.

"I'm kidding. You're adorable. I do need to go, though."

I hugged them both, hugged Badger an extra-long time, sniffing his warm puppy fur, and headed to Cara's apartment.

Was this a terrible idea? Or was I only wondering now because I was sad about leaving my dog? I couldn't decide. But it was only nine days. How big a mistake could it be when it would be finished before the milk in my fridge expired? Wouldn't it? I probably should've checked the date.

But I was already parking and walking to Cara's door, so it seemed too late, both to check the milk and to change my mind.

And the idea of leaving my wedding picture behind, neither looking at it nor being tempted to look at it when I was trying not to look at it, was already making me think maybe I'd made the right choice.

"You're here!" Cara said, wheeling out a suitcase. "Grab your bags. You can move them right from your car to mine."

Cara pressed the remote key in her other hand, and a tiny hatchback across from us opened.

"Your car is very orange," I said.

"Yes. You've seen it before, haven't you?"

"No, I definitely would've remembered. It's like an Orangesicle."

"Yeah, yeah."

"It's like a traffic cone. It's actually not much bigger than a traffic cone, either. Is it a traffic cone pretending to be a car?"

She sighed.

I grinned, unable to stop now that she'd shown she was irritated. I tilted my head, eyeing the car and thinking. "You should put a stem on it for Halloween."

She rolled her eyes. "You know what? I like it. And I never have trouble finding it in the parking lot."

"I bet you don't."

Cara helped me with the cooler, the bag of snacks with Mom's cookies balanced on top, a bag that was mostly charging cords and headphones, and another that was entirely full of books.

When we were finished, I brought out my guitar case.

"I'm not sure there's room," I said, hearing and hating the tentative note in my voice.

"We can make it work," Cara said without hesitation.

She shifted the cooler. I wedged a snack bag against the other door, and somehow, the guitar case fit.

"It is a guitar in there, right? Not like drugs or guns or—"

I had to laugh. "I think it's supposed to be a violin case, if it's a gun. And for drugs, something less conspicuous, like a thousand rubber ducks." I unlocked the case and showed her. "Just a guitar, a strap, a tuner, a Glock, a capo, and an alarming amount of my hair." I picked out a purple strand and shook it off my fingers into the parking lot. "Not even an amp because I figured we definitely wouldn't have room for that."

"What a pity," Cara said sarcastically, and I remembered her Led Zeppelin comment and grinned. "I tried to play the guitar," she added, "but I couldn't figure out where my elbows were supposed to be. It felt awkward as hell. Probably looked awkward, too." She closed the hatchback. There was a faded Houston Audubon sticker on the back with a picture of a black and yellow songbird.

I had the sudden mental image of standing in the same spot while Cara watched a rare red-butted canary for two hours.

"You don't have a fancy camera with a giant lens in there, do you?" I asked. Even I could hear the suspicion in my voice. I sounded like Cara had, asking if there were drugs in my guitar case.

"Nope," she said. "No cameras at all but this one." She held up her phone.

"Good," I said.

We took last-minute bathroom breaks, then we were on the road.

Chapter Eight

It took an hour just to get out of Houston. I spent that time staring at the map on the car monitor. For all that the car was bright orange on the outside, it was comfortable inside, with black seats and plenty of cup holders and USB ports. That was the extent of my car knowledge.

"That is not a straight line." I pointed at the map on the screen.

Cara huffed. "It's a road trip, Honey, not a flight. We have tourist stops, destinations."

"Speaking of which, I'm so glad neither of us wants to go to Disneyland."

"Me, too. I was willing to make compromises, but it would've been me hanging out in the hotel while you went to Disneyland by yourself, and I would've felt guilty."

I imagined Cara in a hotel robe, drink in hand, clicking through the cable channels. "Not too guilty."

"Yeah, you're right. Is it weird that we don't have any destination stops in Texas?"

I thought about it. "No. I mean, we've both lived here for a long time. I'm sure we've seen all the major tourist sites."

"Hmm," she said. "The Alamo?"

"Seen it. Big Bend?"

"Seen it. South Padre Island?"

"Oh," I said, "well, no. But it's a little out of our way."

Cara grinned. "It's worth the drive. Miles and miles of sand, hundreds of seabirds. I saw a starfish once."

"Cool," I said genuinely. I'd never seen a starfish except in the zoo. "I love the beach, but I haven't been since my dog discovered that he can't swim."

"Oh no," she said with a gasp.

"It was fine. I just pulled him up by his leash. The fisherman on the pier did a double take."

"Hah, dogfish," Cara quipped. "What's his name?"

"I assume you mean my dog, not the fisherman. Badger."

She thought about that for a minute. "Badger. You, Honey, have a dog named Badger. That's adorable. Is he a vicious predator?"

"He's a black cotton ball with manic tendencies."

"Do you have a picture?"

I showed her my home screen and she *awww*ed.

"We got him a few months ago. I'd forgotten that you hadn't met him. Have you ever had pets?"

Cara shook her head. "My mom's allergic to every nonhuman mammal she's ever met. I had a goldfish once. Not very exciting."

"Your mom doesn't live nearby, does she? Have you thought about getting a pet now…?" I almost said, now that you live alone, but it felt too sharp. Still, Badger was the only reason my house wasn't lonely.

She shrugged. "I guess I could. Mom's in New Orleans. She never leaves."

"Come meet Badger when we're back home. He'll make up your mind."

Cara smiled, glancing again at my phone screen. "I have no doubt."

As the skyscrapers gave way to box stores, the GPS spoke in a calm, British, male voice. I raised my eyebrows at her.

"Yes, I downloaded a voice for my GPS that sounds like Sir David Attenborough," she said in explanation, not at all apologetic.

I nodded, not confessing that my GPS sounded like Fran Drescher. It had been a joke, but Bridget had been so annoyed that I'd kept it. I was fond of my faux Fran now.

Earlier in the week, Cara had shared a work-in-progress itinerary with me online, titled *Spring Break, Bitches!!!* It made me laugh. I opened it now.

"Nothing of note today except to put our non–spring break life in the rearview mirror," I said. "We'll spend the entire day in the car and barely make it out of Texas. Kind of a bummer, isn't it? Maybe we should've gone east. For morale."

"We have your day one playlist for morale," Cara said. "And day two will be worth it."

"I'll take your word for it."

Cara spared half a second to glance at me. "What are you talking about? You got the itinerary, didn't you?"

"Sure, but I didn't look at it."

Cara gaped. "You didn't look at it? You just got in the car with me and let me just take you wherever?"

I looked her up and down. "Are you a kidnapper? Smuggler? Recruiter for the WNBA?"

"No." Cara's tone said *obviously not.*

"Then I'm probably fine," I said.

Cara drove with that same baffled expression on her face for miles. Unsurprisingly, she also drove the speed limit, with hands at the two and ten positions.

I watched the miles and miles of buildings, intertwining roads, and repetitive billboards until my eyes started to feel heavy. I made myself stay awake until we were out of Houston. I wanted to wish it a silent farewell and fuck off, which I accidentally said out loud.

"Amen," Cara said.

Somewhere in the Texas Hill Country and in the middle of "The Tortured Poets Department," Cara murmuring along with Taylor about being truly known, I fell asleep.

CHAPTER NINE

We took three-hour shifts behind the wheel, sometimes swapping when we stopped for gas, sometimes pulling over next to fields where cows grazed, once near a field of green plants that I thought were cotton. I'd stopped once on a weekend trip to Austin to pick up a boll and feel its strange softness, the lumps of seeds inside.

"It's the fruit, you know," Cara said when I told her.

"What is?"

"The cottony part of the cotton plant. That's the plant's fruit."

"Huh," I said. "Weird."

And we drove on.

Cara never failed to spot a baby cow or goat in the field and say, "Awww! Look, BABIES!"

We talked about the flowers—it was an excellent time for a road trip. Bluebonnets, Indian paintbrushes, and evening primroses filled the grassy medians and ditches. I did internet searches for the ones that I didn't already know, which were…all of them but the bluebonnets.

Cara and I fell silent when we passed fields of sunflowers at sunset.

"Wow," she said finally.

"I've definitely seen uglier places," I said.

She just nodded.

Cara napped, too, during my first driving shift, which surprised me for some reason. I guess I'd imagined her as someone who would sit straight, seat belt perfectly buckled, watching the road in case I missed anything, not leaned back with her sock feet on the dash.

Was I too hard on her? Possibly. But she also wouldn't apply lip balm while driving because it was too distracting, so I can't be blamed.

I twisted my purple streak into a curl, finished off the last of Mom's monster cookies that Cara enjoyed as much as I did, and listened to my playlist as Cara slept, singing along in a whisper, and when I grew bored, I quietly recited the Mary Oliver poems I'd memorized: "Wild Geese" and "Black Oaks" and a prose poem, "May," about encountering a copperhead snake for the first time, in which she doesn't run away screaming like I would but has a profound emotional experience instead. Because…that's Mary Oliver.

Cara would probably run away from a copperhead, too, but she'd also know exactly what species it was and whether it was juvenile or adult and how many eggs it laid, whereas I would just be running because it was snake-shaped.

Cara and I spent the night at a midrange hotel a few miles on the other side, finally, of the Texas-New Mexico border.

I was worried that it would be a little awkward—I hadn't shared a room with anyone but Bridget since college. But there wasn't any time for awkwardness. We played rock, paper, scissors for who had the shower first. I won, and as soon as I was out and mostly dry, I put on my pajamas, brushed my teeth, braided my mass of hair so it wouldn't strangle me in the night, and curled up under the thick duvet.

Cara hadn't even gotten out of the shower before I was asleep.

I was a little embarrassed about how eager I was to see the International UFO Museum and Research Center in Roswell the next day. It wasn't as though I had an *I Want to Believe* poster on my wall. Anymore. But I had read more about this stop than any other that Cara and I had talked about, trying to convince myself that it wasn't worth our time and failing completely.

"How much time do we have scheduled for Roswell?" I asked as I found a parking spot.

"No, we're not doing that," Cara said.

"Doing what?"

"We're not scheduling out our days by the hour. My job runs on a literal bell. I can make my peace with alarm clocks and check-in times, but I'm not going to set a timer for our actual adventures." Her cheeks went faintly pink. "I mean, excursions…destinations…whatever."

"No, I like *adventures*," I said, bumping her shoulder with mine. I'd always had the impression that she was shorter than me, but our shoulders were very nearly even. Huh. "You went with the average amount of time spent here feature on your maps app, didn't you?" I asked as we paid for our tickets.

Cara smiled and tried to hide it. "It's just an estimate, Honey."

"Alright," I teased. "Get ready for fourteen hours of alien evidence."

The elderly man behind the ticket counter said, "We, uh, close at five p.m."

"Did you account for the time dilation associated with light speed travel?" I asked.

Cara grabbed my arm and dragged me inside.

And oh.

This place found the line between believable evidence and outrageous conspiracy theory and played it like a jump rope.

There were staged alien dissections attended by CIA agents in suits and bowler hats, newspaper clippings and photographs of close encounters framed on each wall, and depictions of science fiction aliens through the ages.

I spent entirely too long at a wall with information—quote, unquote *information*—about the first documented alien abduction case in the US and was soon joined by an elderly woman who was eager to tell me about the night that she, too, had been abducted and kept for three years before *they* returned her. They had, of course, left an undetectable tracking device in her belly button.

Cara just stood beside me and sighed loudly and pointedly until the woman left.

Cara wasn't having a terrible time, though. I could tell that she found the tiny papier-mâché aliens charming, and that she was as delighted as I was when the UFO at the center of the room started spinning, lighting up, and emitting fog.

At the end of all the delightful madness was the weirdest gift shop I'd ever seen. I bought Badger an alien costume that he'd hate and bought myself a bobblehead and a bright green alien hunter hard hat with attached light. After half a moment's hesitation, I bought a hard hat for Cara, too.

"Not exactly what I had in mind for our first Mesmio reel, Honey," she said, "but…it's perfect. It's not at all the kind of thing Lorenzo would expect me to do."

We recorded ourselves in front of a life-sized UFO, laughing and switching our headlamps on.

It wasn't a long video. It certainly wasn't anything that would bring us followers.

But, as Cara pointed out, that wasn't the point. The point was that while the exes were on their stupid cruise, we were out having fun too, and if we shared that fact with our loved ones and despised ones, well that was just a bonus.

Down the street, we found Alien Zone and paid our three dollars each to pose with aliens wearing boxer shorts in a 1980s-style dorm room, then sitting in an outhouse. Cara and I took turns on the examination table while a plastic alien medic loomed over us. And we played foosball with another. Halfway through, we were laughing so hard that neither of us could operate our legs properly, let alone post to Mesmio. We had to give it up until we recovered.

We sat at the bar with the alien bartender, telling him our troubles and appreciating his terrific listening skills.

"If only all men were like you," Cara crooned, leaning over to adjust his bow tie.

"Silent, attentive, and can make a cocktail?" I asked.

Cara thought about it. "Yes. And such a snazzy dresser."

I dragged Cara away from the bar and into a UFO, where we posted more reels and shared the valuable lessons we'd learned about not tempting fate by standing under tractor beams next to cows at night.

I checked Bridget's Mesmio page while I had the app open. "No new posts from Bridget and Lorenzo today."

"I'm sorry," Cara said. "I don't know anyone by those names."

She said it with sass and a hair flip. I rolled my eyes.

"So," I said as we headed back to the car. "What did you think of the museum? Are you convinced that there's life out there?"

Cara shook her head. "I'm convinced that the people of Roswell have found a lucrative hobby."

"Skeptic," I said, making my new alien bobblehead mimic her head shake.

❖

Later, while Cara filled up the gas tank, I browsed convenience store snacks and stretched my sore back. Sitting in a car shouldn't hurt, but I supposed I wasn't twenty anymore.

My phone vibrated in my pocket. I glanced at the screen and answered.

"Happy Maha Shivaratri, Honey."

"I'm not Hindu, Dad. And neither are you."

"Don't tell me what I'm not. I could be Hindu."

"Are you?" I grabbed a mini roll of Oreos, then put them back and grabbed the family size.

"No. But I believe we should all coexist. Each to their om."

"Dad…"

"Do you know why we pray to Lord Ganesha?"

"Please stop."

"We have to address the elephant in the room!"

"Let me talk to Mom."

There was a muffled shuffling sound and my mother's voice, "I'm never letting your father talk to your Uncle Farid again. They were on the phone for over an hour last night, and I thought your father was going to laugh until he suffocated."

From the background, Dad said, "A Hindu swami, a Jewish rabbi, and a Catholic priest walk into a bar. The bartender says, *What is this, a joke?*" Then he laughed until I could hear him start to wheeze, unable to catch his breath.

"God help us. Seriously," Mom said.

"Do you need to go check on him?"

"Maybe. But if he passes out, at least I'll get a break from the world's worst religious comedian."

"That's kind of a mouthful. I think I'll just keep calling him *Dad*."

Mom yelled, "Go get your inhaler, nitwit."

"That works, too. How's Badger?"

"An angel. Aren't you, fluffy puff?" Her voice devolved into baby talk.

I heard his happy panting in the background and was surprised by how acutely I missed him. I wasn't one of those people who referred to their pets as their fur babies or maxed out their credit cards buying him outfits. Badger was, indeed, a sweet little fluffy puff, but he didn't notice or care who was taking care of him. He even seemed to prefer my parents, so they could all just have each other. Jerks.

"How's the trip going so far?" Mom asked carefully.

"It's great," I answered a little fiercely. "It's fun to be with someone who doesn't keep trying to feed me and convince me to move into my childhood bedroom."

"I'm sorry for loving you so much."

I laughed. "You sound like Grandma Singh."

"Are you accusing me of stealing phrases from my mother-in-law, the world expert on guilt trips? Yes. Yes, I did. But you're really having a good time? You know I worry."

"I know you do," I said, moving to the register. "But it's been really nice, actually. I'm already tired of being in the car, but the drive has been beautiful."

"And your friend?"

I sighed. "I'm not tired of Cara. Yet."

She had come into the convenience store and was standing beside me, grinning, holding up her family-size pack of Oreos to show that we'd picked out the same thing. When she heard me, she dropped her smile and pretended to be offended.

"She drives like there's a cop around every fucking corner," I complained. "Not one mile over the speed limit, the whole way. This trip is going to take forever."

"What a monster," Mom said blandly.

"Yeah, well," Cara said, leaning toward the phone, "Honey drives like—"

"Oops, sorry Mom. Going through a tunnel. Call you later." I hung up.

Chapter Ten

We weren't far from our next adventure. Sir David Attenborough's voice on the GPS no longer gave us irritating directions like "*For the next one hundred thirty-four miles, stay on US-87 North.*" No one needs that bullshit, not even from Dave.

White Sands National Park had made both of our lists.

Cara and I picked up some tacos in Alamogordo, and I ate while I drove, despite Cara's repeated reminder that I could just pull over.

"If it was a better taco, it would be worth my concentration," I said. "As it is, the road is more interesting than what's happening in my mouth."

The road was completely straight and empty. Maybe New Mexico didn't have spring break this week.

Cara and I had exhausted our chitchat, but she had, true to her word, made a list of conversation topics to keep us occupied on the drive.

"I'm sorry," I said to Beyoncé as I turned down "Texas Hold 'Em."

Cara ignored me. "What are your favorite things about yourself?"

"Skip."

"I am not a CD player, and that's not how this works."

I pouted.

"Come on," she said. "This isn't even a hard one. I'll go first. I like that I'm curious." She stared at me as I drove, as though expecting me to roll my eyes. When I didn't, she went on, "I think it's something most people have, but most people lose as they grow up. All those questions—why is the sky blue, what happened to the dinosaurs, how much salt is in the ocean?"

"Nerd questions," I pointed out.

"Exactly," Cara said. "I want the facts. I want the answers. Some people say they were born in the wrong era. Not me. I need to google."

I laughed. "Okay, I can understand that. But that's really what you like most? Not your intelligence or your humor or…I don't know, your curls? I don't want to be shallow, but you have some pretty amazing curls."

Her cheeks reddened, just a smidge. "I like those things, too, but if I had to pick one…"

"Curiosity."

"Curiosity," she confirmed. "Okay, now you."

I could tell she was eager to get the focus off her, so I played along. "There are *so many* options."

Cara shook her head in sympathy. "How will you ever choose?"

"You picked something all deep and thoughtful. I can't just say I like my purple hair."

"I mean, you can. I will judge you, though."

I laughed. "I like…music."

"That's not an answer."

"Let me finish, Impatient McJudgy. It's maybe not a surprise that music is a big part of my life. I can still remember…Never mind, that's a long story. I don't have to tell it. The answer is that my connection to music—"

"Tell it," Cara interrupted again.

"What?"

"Oh no, wait. I do have a meeting I need to get to." She looked pointedly at the miles of empty road ahead of us, then back at me, blandly demanding, "Tell the story."

For a moment, I stared at the road, wondering when was the last time I'd been invited to talk about myself, my life, with someone who actually wanted to listen.

As if to make a point, Cara stopped talking altogether and waited.

"Okay," I started, then kept looking ahead, thinking. "Okay," I tried again. "When I was in middle school, I had a Savage Garden CD."

Cara squeaked. Literally squeaked, then went quiet again.

"I assume that the mouse in the passenger's seat also had a Savage Garden CD?"

She nodded with enough enthusiasm that I knew she would understand the rest of the story as well as anyone else could.

"So, I had been singing 'Truly Madly Deeply' along with all my preteen friends for weeks. I finally talked Mom into buying me the CD, which she did only because I swore I'd use the headphones I hated. I preferred to loudly share my music with the whole household, and Mom's never been a nineties pop fan. And to be fair, it's not the most musically or lyrically sophisticated song, right?"

Cara nodded.

"Right after the last verse, one of the vocalists whispers—and it was hardly noticeable when I played it through the speakers, but unmistakable through the headphones—a breathy, quickly whispered *I love you.*"

Cara put her hands over her mouth, and I knew that she knew exactly what I was talking about.

"It gave me fucking chills. Not metaphorically. I had a physical reaction. Not my last, when it comes to love songs. And like I said, this isn't a masterpiece. But I caught a glimpse of what music could do, and I was awestruck. Right then, I started begging for piano lessons, and I was very, very lucky to have parents who…well, for all that they were brass players, they understood the feeling."

Cara didn't rush to fill the silence after my words, but after a minute, she said, not in a critical tone, but just as though she wanted to be sure she understood, "That's what you like most about yourself? Your love of music?"

"I think…I like that I'm a part of it. Like, as a woman, I'm a part of the history of womanness, in my own small way. It's something I understand and belong to and also get to be a part of making and telling that story. I also understand and belong to and create music."

After a moment, Cara let out a breath that sounded a little like, "Wow."

Then she was quiet again for a long time, as though thinking about what I'd said, and I wanted to interrupt, to make a joke, but also, I wanted to keep the silence, to think about what she and I had both said, and about how and why I felt so breathless.

What did it say about my marriage that this was the first moment in years when I felt heard? There was something about the opened-up feeling that stripped away some of the loneliness I'd hardly noticed building up inside me.

We kept driving.

We were quiet, with the music still playing softly in the background, but it wasn't Beyoncé anymore, and as the first rap song on my list started, Cara looked at the stereo with a dubious expression.

It was close enough to our usual time to switch drivers, so I told her to pull over.

"Are you kicking me out?" she asked. "I didn't say a word about your music."

"It's your car, you…very nice person," I said.

"You were just about to insult me, weren't you? It's okay. I can take it."

I looked right into her eyes. "Your taste in music isn't optimal. But you're still very pretty. Now listen."

While she pulled us back onto the road, I scrolled to a rap song I was sure she'd like. Dessa's familiar voice filled the car. I turned up the volume.

We listened to "Fighting Fish" on repeat until we could get through the whole thing, Cara singing the chorus, and me rapping the verses.

We were loud and terrible, and it reminded me of high school lunches after the latest Britney Spears album dropped. Our table kept the whole cafeteria entertained, and I'd adored every moment. Maybe I needed to start up a Strings & Things choir club.

"I really admire that she can rhyme *bitch* and *fish* and pull it off," Cara said. "That's a rare talent."

"She has kind of an obsession with dice and luck, too. Listen to this one." I started "5 Out of 6," which Cara liked even more, and followed that with every other Dessa song I'd downloaded, including her song on *The Hamilton Mixtape*.

"Oh, oh, oh," Cara said. We had to listen to that one several times. "This song always makes me wish I had a sister."

"Same," I said. "Though I don't think I'm enough like Angelica to be so devoted or enough like Eliza to deserve it."

Cara glanced at me. "I don't know about that. I saw you with Bridget. You were very Angelica. And I definitely think you deserve Eliza-level devotion."

Her voice had that tone to it that women in my life always seemed to take when they were encouraging each other, the Girl Power or Womanly Solidarity tone, the *no bullshit quirky friend teaching the main character to respect herself* tone.

"You underappreciate yourself," she said. "You deserve every good thing, Honey."

"A billion dollars?"

Cara sighed and said, "Yeah," but it was the *yeah* of the defeated. She knew I was being an ass.

"Cake?" I asked.

"Yeah."

"What about one of those T. rex skulls for decoration, the kind they put glass on so it also works as a side table?"

"God, no. I take it back."

I laughed, then played "Fighting Fish" again. We sang until we reached White Sands.

❖

We parked at the visitors' center for maps, restroom breaks, and a sled that Cara took one look at and said, "Nope."

"Come on," I said. "It's bright orange. You love bright orange."

"I also like my bones unbroken."

I ignored her. The sled, more of a shallow bowl in shape than what I'd normally call a sled, barely fit on top of our luggage and my guitar case in the back seat.

There was one other car in the parking area near the dunes, a minivan with sunburned, windswept children piling inside to leave. We really did have the place to ourselves. I changed into shorts that showed off my awesome guitar tattoo with watercolor-style rainbow strings and an olive green T-shirt. It clashed with my purple hair, but I loved the fit. I'd been wearing my hair loose, but now I braided it tightly.

Cara was flipping through a brochure. She was wearing a cream sundress with a lacy belt. It was definitely going to fly over her head in this wind, but since there was no one around but me, I didn't bother pointing it out.

"Did you know that the sand is gypsum?" she asked, pointing at a line in the brochure. "That's why it's cool to the touch even when it's hot outside."

"Mm-hmm," I said and unloaded the sled.

"Wow, there are forty-five species that only live within the national park."

"Really?" The place seemed huge, but not big enough for that.

"Most of them are moths."

"Ugh, okay. Let's go."

Cara was still straightening a wide-brimmed hat that she'd somehow located in the back seat when I started climbing the nearest dune.

My feet sank into the powdery sand, and I immediately kicked my shoes in the general direction of the car. Badger would've been rolling all over, getting sandy and matted and having a blast.

"I apologize," I said to the dunes. "You are so much more than a sealess beach."

The dune was easily taller than a two-story building. I hopped on the sled at the top with anticipation in my stomach and held on tight.

I slid. Slowly.

Cara watched me from the bottom, grinning under her massive sun hat.

I wiggled. I ducked low to be more streamlined. I was moving, picking up a little speed as I went down, but nothing like I'd imagined. I could've leisurely drunk an espresso on the way down without spilling a drop.

"I just realized that all my sledding expectations come from cartoon characters sledding in the snow," I said as I neared the bottom.

Cara tilted her head. "You've never gone sledding in the snow?"

"In Houston? I managed to build a six-inch-tall snowman. Once."

"No, obviously not in Houston, Honey," she said, exasperated again. It was amazing how easily I could exasperate her. I just had to be myself.

"My family never vacationed much," I said, "and I guess I kept up the tradition."

Cara shook her head. "Honey, if we don't kill each other by the end of this, we'll spend fall break in the Rocky Mountains."

"Cara Espinoza," I said, standing and lifting the sled. "It's a date." I tilted the sled toward her. "Your turn?"

"For that roller coaster? You bet."

Cara ran up the dunes in her sandals, and I followed her, grinning.

At the top, I held the sled while she sat cross-legged inside. Then I pushed her. Hard.

In my defense…I can't think of an acceptable excuse for my behavior, and I'm sure Cara would agree that it was uncalled for. I just thought of her grinning at my snail-slow descent, and I pushed.

She didn't have a firm grip on the edge of the sled, and as it slid forward, she tilted backward. She flipped off the back, and when she landed, she just kept rolling, her shoes flying off, her sundress bunching around her waist, showing off lacy white panties.

I stood for a moment in shock as she tumbled down toward the bottom of the dune. Then I ran as fast as I could, slipping and landing on my ass in the sand repeatedly.

She reached the bottom, sat up, and looked at me racing down after her with the horror I felt clear in my face. I felt a little better, just seeing her move. I'd already started to fast-forward to a hospital room where a doctor explained that the spinal injury was likely permanent, and it would be my responsibility to feed her for the rest of her life because I'd pushed her down the goddamned dune like an attempted murderer.

Cara watched me descend. Her sun hat had flown off somewhere, and the fine sand stuck to her arms and legs and face.

Then she laughed, pulling her sundress back down. "Let's do it again," she called out.

Before I could reach her, she was racing to where the sled had landed. She lifted it over her head and started climbing as fast as she could back to the top.

I stood for a moment, my heart still racing, listening to her laugh. I'd expected her to shout at me. I'd thought of Cara as the uptight one, the one who cared whether her sock drawer was organized, but I may have been wrong.

The sound of her laughter was better than music. It was permission to sweep the eggshells out from under my feet.

Without wanting to, I thought of Bridget, of how any misstep of mine on the dance floor had surely broken her toe, of how any accident, however small, meant the end of the fun for her, meant leaving parties early, especially if they were parties with *my* friends, meant that she needed painkillers and an ice pack and a quiet room, so I could sleep on the couch.

I hated that couch. We'd bought it together when she moved in, and I'd never thought about it, but suddenly, I hated it with more passion than any piece of furniture had a right to spark in me. It was hideous—striped, hard, and narrow.

I followed Cara to the top, and this time I asked, "Holding on tight?"

"Yes."

"And you want me to actually push you hard?"

"Yes."

"And I'm sorry."

For a moment, Cara sat with her hands gripped onto the edge, her dark hair a tangled, sandy mess.

Then she said, "I think I can trust you to see when I need to be pushed. Does that make sense?"

I wasn't sure that it did. But I pushed anyway.

As she slid down the hill, faster than I had but not actually very fast, she leaned into the slide and laughed all the way down.

I grinned at her, and when she reached the bottom, she started climbing back up, yelling, "Your turn!"

When we had each taken a dozen turns sledding, we took a water break, then decided to explore.

Honestly, I hadn't looked around much when we arrived. Sledding had been my top priority.

I hadn't known that I was missing the view.

Mountains, blue in the distance, surrounded the sands, and there was nothing between here and there but those pristine white dunes and the occasional spiky bush or patch of brown, dry-looking grass.

"We could walk for days and not get to the edge," Cara said, her voice soft in the breeze. "It's technically a desert, but there's no desert in the world quite like it."

I heard her words and let them settle over me. I was truthful when I said that my family never traveled much. We couldn't afford it. And once I was an adult, each rare windfall had gone into savings for the store.

My parents had started traveling again once they retired, just a little, and I'd found myself strangely jealous. I did want to see the world, and I didn't really want to wait until my knees hurt before I could.

But in my mind, *seeing the world* meant buying a thousand-dollar plane ticket out of the country, seeing Abbey Road, Musikverein in Vienna, and Seoul, the birthplace of K-pop. I'd been to the SXSW music festival in Austin, but it hadn't occurred to me that a place as unique as White Sands could be so near, that there was so much seeing the world I could do in a little over a day's drive.

The sun was setting when we remembered to record a Mesmio reel. By that time, we were exhausted and sweaty, but we still looked excellent on camera in the golden light. Cara was a shade darker in complexion, her eyes brighter, but when I looked at myself on the screen, I was surprised to see how widely I was smiling, how alive my eyes looked, too.

Cara shared a few fun facts, then added in a clip of me taking one last spinning sled trip down the highest dune we'd found.

We took some time brushing sand off and out of our clothes and hair when we got back to the car. Neither of us liked the idea of carrying any of it with us through the days of travel ahead.

We opened the cooler and grabbed snacks and drinks for the next part of the drive. Cara opened her tenth bag of popcorn, white cheddar this time. It smelled like last week's socks, but she seemed happy, so I didn't complain.

"How far is the hotel for tonight?" I asked, trying but not succeeding in keeping the whine from my voice. If it was going to be another late night, I was going to struggle to stay awake for my driving shift.

"Twenty miles," she said. "And there's fast food on the way."

"Bless you," I said, "and just for that, you can have the first shower."

"I can have it first tonight because you had it first last night," she corrected.

"Fine. Reject my generosity. Just feed me soon."

"Yes, ma'am," she said and started the car.

Chapter Eleven

The hotel was nice enough that I took notice, tired as I was.

"This place," I said as we dropped fast food wrappers into the trash can and hauled luggage to the elevator.

"Fancy, right? I got a last-minute deal you wouldn't believe." Cara seemed pleased that I'd noticed.

"That's…thank you. Thank you for taking care of all the planning. It's hitting me how little I did to prepare for this trip, compared with you."

Her smile widened. "You are very welcome. I enjoy the planning part. There were times with Lorenzo that I enjoyed the planning more than the vacation itself."

"I get that," I said. And I did. Even on weekend trips with Bridget, I'd find that I enjoyed the travel snacks more than the company.

As Cara took out the key card for the door, everything I'd said today came to mind at once. Had I been unhappy? I didn't know if I could trust my memories right now. I was still too angry to think clearly. But I did myself the favor of not disregarding what I felt, just setting it aside to examine when I was less exhausted.

"If you like the hotel now," Cara said, "just wait until breakfast."

I called the store while Cara showered. I tried to stay near the door and not get sand in the room, but I soon gave up and sat at the desk, reasoning that so long as I didn't get sand in the beds, Cara couldn't be too upset with me.

Doug answered, "Strings & Things, Douglas speaking."

I snickered, then tried to cover it with a cough. "Hey, Doug. It's Honey. How's it going?"

"That drum kit finally sold. I thought we'd never get rid of it. I hate those effing cymbals."

I was impressed. That was a good sale. "Yeah," I said, "but you know we're just going to get another one, right? If it helps, there are bongos in the next delivery."

"*Coooool.* Hey, can wireless mics go bad? We have one that smells weird."

"Weird like it's going to burst into flames? Or weird like someone breathed into it a lot—maybe someone who doesn't floss?"

There was a gagging sound on the line, then Florence took the phone.

"Honey, stop calling and worrying about us," she said. "Your body needs a break, but your brain does, too. We've got this."

"I know you do. I actually haven't been worried at all." It was strange to think that was almost true. I missed the store, but I was pretty sure Florence and Doug were better at running it than I was.

"Good," she said. "Now be sure to have some fun, get into a little trouble, then tell me all about it. In detail, if you please."

I heard the shower stop and immediately stood.

"I have to go, Florence," I said. "Cara's…" I didn't want to say *Cara's getting out of the shower* because Florence had a tendency to take innocent statements and make them weird, so I lied. "Cara's waiting."

"Whatever cranks your tractor, Hon. She is a pretty one."

I put my head in my free hand. "What…? Never mind, please don't tell me what that means. I'll call again tomorrow."

"Or don't," Florence singsonged. "Your choice."

Cara was so very right about breakfast. There was a hot buffet, a made-to-order omelet station, and a coffee bar on top of the usual continental breakfast offerings.

I'd stayed in a hotel once that offered cereal and milk and black coffee and called it breakfast.

For the moment, I didn't care if Cara and I had paid full price and a half for this place. We sat at a table next to an indoor fountain, surrounded by tropical plants. Soft music played, interspersed with nature sounds. There weren't many other guests, but they all looked as calm as I felt, drifting to their tables with mountains of food.

I had two delicious platefuls, and so did Cara: waffles with whipped cream and berries, omelets with every meat and vegetable they offered, and entirely too much bacon. We drank cappuccinos until we were jittery. We were children on vacation, grabbing one last chocolate muffin on our way out the door.

"We could just stay here," I said.

Cara shrugged. "It wouldn't be a bad place to spend the week."

"I meant forever," I said, and she laughed.

We made a couple of Mesmio reels on the road, making up dances to my music mix and telling jokes, most of them stupid.

"There were two muffins in an oven," I said. "One muffin turns to the other muffin and says, 'Damn, it's hot in here.' The second muffin says, 'Aaah! A talking muffin!'"

Cara's pity laugh got me laughing, too.

"Why does Snoop Dogg carry an umbrella?" she asked.

"Why?"

"Fo' drizzle," she said, then laughed uproariously.

"More than half of Mesmio users are too young to understand that joke."

"Oh, oh!" Cara said excitedly. "Do you want to hear the first recorded joke in the English language? What hangs at a man's thigh and wants to poke the hole that it's often poked before?"

I faked a gasp, trying not to laugh, "Cara!"

"A key," she said, grinning. "Mind out of the gutter, Honey." She winked at her phone and ended the recording.

I burst out laughing.

"We have some new followers," Cara said.

"Anyone you know?" I wanted to ask if Lorenzo and Bridget were following us, of course. I wanted to hear that they had commented, saying that they had clearly been wrong, that we were the loves of their lives, that they wanted, no, needed us to come home.

For a moment, I let that fantasy fester. I imagined holding Bridget again. I imagined her in her blush ball gown at our wedding. I imagined trying to love her and trust her, but knowing that she had chosen someone else.

The reality was that she had walked out, and for the first time, I honestly couldn't imagine taking her back. Even under all the anger, I hadn't reached the point of being glad she was gone. But I was a step closer.

I tried to turn my attention back to Cara, who was reading out Mesmio handles. "No one I recognize," she said.

"Well, we are fucking delightful."

"And charming."

Cara replayed our Mesmio reel from Roswell, and we both laughed at our hard hats, already lost somewhere in the back seat.

"Oh, look at this comment," she said, not holding up the phone to show me because I was driving, but getting ready to read it aloud.

"Don't read the comments. What are you, new to the internet?"

"It's sweet," she said. "*How long have you two been together?* Hashtag #relationshipgoals."

I nodded sagely. "Alien autopsies have always been part of my relationship goals, too."

She kept reading. "*Looks like so much fun. Makes me crave a road trip.* And *I heart you, Cara and Honey.* And *The busty one with the purple hair is hot. I'd let her take me to space.*"

"Ew," I said, "and what?"

Cara laughed. I knew she had to be skimming and skipping the gross and rude comments and just reading me the nice ones. It was sweet.

"This one just says, *Bidi Bidi Bom Bom*."

Now I was laughing. "Because you look like Selena!"

"The Latina singer? You know I'm white, right?"

I looked at her, my mouth falling open.

She laughed. "I'm kidding. Well, mostly. My grandmother is Irish."

"Aren't you supposed to be redheaded and freckled, lass?"

Cara grinned. "My father was Irish and Puerto Rican. My mother's family was originally from Mexico and has lived in New Orleans for seven generations. We can all cook enchiladas *and* boudin."

"Well," I said, "you still look a lot like Selena."

Cara pulled down the visor and looked in the mirror. "No way," she said.

"How can you not see it? I'm buying you some red lipstick next time we stop. You'll see."

I glanced over at her again, watching her pout her luscious lips in the mirror. The rest of her could be as attractive as Badger's butt, and it would still be difficult to ignore those lips. Her tongue flicked out to moisten them, and I…I had to focus on keeping the car inside the lines.

For a moment, I let myself imagine the feel of her mouth against my throat and had to take a few deep breaths, quietly, so she didn't realize the effect she was having on me.

"Don't worry," I said, trying and failing not to glance over again. "It's a compliment."

"Being compared to Selena? Of course it's a compliment."

Then she shocked me so completely that I almost drove off the road, pursing her lips briefly for the mirror and breaking out in a perfect, full volume rendition of "Bidi Bidi Bom Bom."

Chapter Twelve

"Do your parents ever cook Indian food?" Cara asked.

We had a six-hour drive ahead of us, according to Sir David Attenborough, and not much to see besides scrubby desert. From the way Cara had her seat leaned back and her hands behind her head, I figured that she felt like I did, tired from travel, but more relaxed the farther we got down the road. There weren't many days in my adult life when I felt completely free from all responsibility. Besides, you know, not driving into a ditch.

"Only my dad is Indian," I said, "and he is very proud of his ability to scramble an egg. Indian cuisine is a little out of his range. My mom is an excellent cook, but unless it's something you can find at a steakhouse or a grocery store bakery, she's not going to try. In her case, I don't think she lacks skill, just an adventurous culinary spirit."

She raised her eyebrows at my word choice. I knew because I glanced at her as I said it, then turned quickly back to the road.

"Huh, okay," she said.

"Do your parents cook at all?" I asked.

"My dad did a lot before he died last year. Yes, condolences accepted and all that. Basically his cooking is the only thing I miss. He was kind of an ass. My mom is brilliant in the kitchen. Really, you'll have to come with me sometime when I visit. Have you ever had truly amazing Cajun food? Let me rephrase that, have you ever had five times the amount of truly amazing Cajun food that you can possibly eat, and eaten it anyway?"

I laughed. "No, but I'm definitely tagging along to your mom's house."

"Her calas are my favorite breakfast, ever, and I have had literal dreams about her pompano en papillote."

"Why is my mouth watering? I don't even know what those things are."

"You don't, but your future self knows and is broadcasting the joy backward in time to your taste buds. That's how good it is."

I laughed.

"Now for the important question," Cara said. "How did you meet Badger?"

"Oh, the real love of my life? The one who didn't borrow my shirts and then assume they were hers when she moved out?"

"I don't think you and Badger wear the same size."

"Bridget and I didn't either. She's half my size, but that never stopped her."

Cara rolled her eyes. "Are you going to answer my question?"

"What was…? Oh, when I met Badger. Well, it was a dark and stormy night."

"Of course it was."

"I was just getting home from work, and it was pitch black outside. Our neighborhood has lighting problems even when the power's working, and a strong breeze is enough to take out the rest."

"Yes, I'm familiar. I also live in Houston. So, what happened?"

I thought for a moment, reliving the memory. "I tripped over a wet gremlin."

"Aww," Cara said.

"Yes. Aww. I scraped a knee and both elbows, and I lost my umbrella. But there was the gremlin, licking my face. I was pretty sure it was a dog."

"What else would it have been?"

"Rat. Possum. Baby raccoon."

"*Ooookay.*"

"So I picked it up, and it was very wiggly, but I got it into the house, and Bridget said, *There aren't enough shots in the world.*"

"Like vaccines? Or like vodka?"

"You know, I never asked. Let's say both."

"So, Badger…?" she said.

"I washed it, and it turned out to be a dog!" I made jazz hands. Or one jazz hand. The other was on the steering wheel.

"No way," Cara said flatly.

"Yes way. It took about ten seconds of being clean before Bridget decided she loved him and that he was ours forever."

"But you named him," Cara guessed.

"Yes, Bridget wanted to name him something stupid."

"Spot? Max? Shadow?"

"Yes, can you believe that? I gave her two options."

"What was the other?"

I glanced at her, relaxed and smiling in the passenger seat, putting a single jelly bean into her mouth at a time. "BBQ Chicken."

Cara snorted and almost choked on a jelly bean.

When Cara dozed off an hour later, I dug my earbuds out of my pocket and called my parents.

"How's Badger?"

"A perfect little snuggle muffin," Mom said. "How are you and your…friend?"

"We're fine, Mother. Thanks for the hesitation there. Cara *is* my friend, and aren't you always saying you wish I'd take more days off? I'm taking them. Because of her."

She sighed. "I know. It's just strange, thinking of the two of you out there, and your partners off together. It's just…I just—"

"Here, I'm sending you the link to the Mesmio page we're making about our trip. You can see that we're having a wonderful time. Not moping at all." I reminded myself to send the link when we stopped. I didn't think Cara would appreciate waking up to me weaving all over the road.

"Okay, dear," Mom said. "I will take a look. And I do appreciate the pictures you've sent. You look like you're really having fun, and I'm glad. She is adorable, your friend. Isn't she?"

"Cute as a button, Florence says."

Mom laughed. "Florence is the best. Maybe I'll go by and check on the store today."

"So long as you don't let her think that's what you're doing, she'll be happy to see you. She thinks I'm worried about leaving the store with her and Doug."

"Which you're not," she said knowingly.

"No, I'm not," I insisted.

"Except, you are, just a little, because even though they are both very good at their jobs, it's still your business, your store. Not theirs."

"Of course," I admitted. "So you'll text me after you drop by the store?"

"Of course," she mimicked, laughing a little. "You know, you really can still have your old room back if you need it."

"Are you just going to keep dropping that into conversations?"

"There's nothing much in there but a couple of yoga mats and your dad's puzzles. Wouldn't take twenty minutes to get it ready for you."

I rolled my eyes. "Thank you, and no. Not unless it turns out that I really don't have a choice. Like I get home and discover that Godzilla stepped on my house."

"I won't take that personally."

"Because you know that I don't mean it personally. I love you, and *you* know that we started getting along a lot better the day I moved out."

She sighed again. "I know. But I also miss you. Even the fighting."

"Well, I don't miss the fighting. But I will also try to visit more now that…my social schedule has become a little more open."

"I know that you're not supposed to badmouth your child's ex, just in case they make up, but Bridget is a sack of shit, and I hate her."

"Thanks, Mom."

"You're welcome, Honey. Go. Keep enjoying your trip."

"Kiss the little snuggle muffin for me," I said, feeling the bite of missing him.

"Only constantly," she said.

We said our good-byes, and I turned on my music, glancing over at Cara sleeping with her mouth wide open.

I grinned. Cute as a button.

❖

"So, your birth name is Honoria?" Cara asked when she had properly woken up.

"Yes," I said.

It was Cara's turn to drive, and I was using the opportunity to stretch my legs out as far as I could. Driving sucked, and we probably wouldn't even bother stopping for lunch after our hotel breakfast smorgasbord, so it was going to suck for many hours consecutively.

"I was named after my grandmother," I said, "who was deathly ill when I was in utero but recovered miraculously once the birth certificate was signed. She's still fine, living just outside of Vegas with a professional blackjack dealer and their six rescue dogs."

Cara laughed. "Dear goodness. Does she go by *Honey*, too?"

I scoffed. "No, no one would dare, not even my grandpa when he was alive. She is *Honoria* and nothing else. She doesn't even want to be called *grandma*."

"You, on the other hand…"

"I hate the name. Honestly, I hate the nickname, too, but it was kind of inevitable."

She thought about that. "You could've insisted that people call you Nora. Or Nori, like seaweed."

I opened my mouth, then closed it. Had I really never considered that? There was a brief time in middle school when I tried to get everyone to call me Amy because it was an easy-to-spell, easy-to-say, not weird name. But there were four other Amys in my grade, so it's not a surprise that it didn't take.

"You majored in music?" she asked.

"We're just speeding through my childhood here," I said.

She managed to give me an *I'm waiting* expression without taking her eyes off the road.

"I…double majored," I said.

"In…?"

"Music. And accounting."

"Accounting," she said, then gasped. "Oh my God, Honey, are you an accountant?"

"I *was* an accountant."

"But you're all like certified and all that? Can you help me with my taxes?"

"Shut. Up."

She cackled.

"What about you?" I asked. "Education?"

It took her a second or two to finish laughing at me, but then she answered, "Biology with a seven-to-twelfth life science certification."

"Exciting. You went to college with Lorenzo and Bridget, right? University of Houston?"

Cara nodded. "I was a couple years behind them, but yeah. Bridget and I had some friends in common, so when she and Lorenzo organized a fundraising party for an LGBT+ charity, I went and met them both."

"You went?" I asked, then bit my lip.

"You can ask me questions, too, Honey."

"You went as *L*, *G*, *B*, *T*, or plus?"

Cara snorted. "I don't know if that was smooth or stupid. I'm bi. So's Lorenzo. You knew that, right?"

"Yeah, Bridget and I gossiped about Lorenzo, just never about you."

"Thanks?"

"Oh my God," I said, so suddenly that Cara turned away from the road to look at me. "So in our little rainbow troupe, I'm the only True Lesbian?"

Cara gave an exasperated sigh. "Don't call us that, and put down your trophy. Lorenzo and I gossiped about you and Bridget, both."

I laughed. "Okay, fair enough. I've been attracted to men. It just turns out I don't really like them."

"Except…"

"Except what?"

Cara was holding her hand out, as though waiting for me to put an answer in it. "There's always an exception."

"Fine. Except for Alan Alda."

"The guy on *M*A*S*H*? That's who you'd date? He's really old."

I sighed, leaning my head against the passenger window. "Not now. In the seventies. *Young* Hawkeye."

"So your only exception is a time-travel romance with a fictional Korean War doctor?"

"Can I have my fucking trophy back?"

"No."

I blew a raspberry, and she laughed at me.

I'd met Bridget after college, at a club that was frequented by large numbers of senior citizens. At first, I'd been sure that I was at the wrong place. I was meeting up with friends from work, fellow accountants. I spotted only one of them, right in the middle of the dance floor in a plaid shirt and jeans, line dancing with the best of them.

It's not that I was opposed to line dancing. On the contrary, it looked like fun and not too difficult for a newbie. But I had twisted my ankle in Mom's garden a few days before and had only agreed to a night out because I was craving a real martini and because several people from work had planned to meet here and hang out.

No one but Line Dancing Larry showed up.

I ended up at a table near a woman in a sunflower-print dress, her hair hanging loose past her waist. I'd never forget that. Bridget had cut it soon after, and it was beautiful then, too, but that day, she was like a real-life Rapunzel, without the creepy recluse vibes.

I'd been eyeing her when a tall, skinny, dark-haired guy in a cowboy hat came over and pulled her toward the dance floor. She had grinned at him, but when her eyes caught mine, they stayed there for a moment, time stretching out impossibly, until Lorenzo pulled her a second time.

Bridget stayed with him for one dance, and when she went to sit down again, someone else had taken her table. So she sat at mine.

Even then, it was clear how much she loved Lorenzo. I told myself that it was a sibling-type love, and Bridget told me the same. Still, sometimes they would laugh together at their own jokes, hands held and arms entangled, and I had to remind myself. After all, there had been no reason they shouldn't be together then, if they'd wanted to be. They were both single. They'd been friends their whole lives.

Part of me, when I was being very, very generous, could sympathize with what they both must have gone through over the years, realizing that they had either been lying to themselves or each other, or maybe just changing as the years passed, as they recognized the future they had given up by marrying other people.

Lorenzo and Cara moved in together weeks after Bridget and I got married, and after that, everything was different. We had dinner at their house every few months, and they came to ours, but their friendship was an ember of what it had been in college.

Until it wasn't anymore.

I told Cara the story now as we drove through a small town

square, every building straight out of a 1950s movie set. I left out my observations on their difficult friends-to-lovers journey because I didn't want to seem sympathetic to the lying, cheating trash bastards.

"Do you ever…" Cara said, then stopped, not taking her eyes from the traffic light ahead. "Never mind."

"No, what?"

"No, really. It was a horrible question."

"I won't judge you. I promise. Keep in mind that I'm the person who just asked if you were *L*, *G*, *B*, *T*, or plus."

Cara grinned, but it didn't last. "Bridget," she said. "Do you think that's part of why…?"

"No," I said, but I said it gently. "I don't get to blame her cheating on her sexuality. We're all real people. Real choices, real mistakes—"

"Real assholes. I know," she said.

"Yes," I confirmed. "Real assholes, both of them."

Cara nodded, but she still looked sad.

"You can have the trophy for Best Bi if you want it." I handed her an imaginary trophy.

Eyes never leaving the road, she took it with an emotional gasp and held it to her chest. "I'd like to thank the cast of the 1990s movie *The Mummy*…"

"Hilarious," I deadpanned. "Okay, back to your education-and-whatever degree. Did you always want to teach?"

"I always…didn't know what I wanted to do. I figured if I *could* teach, that would at least be a clear career path. Mostly my goal was to not have to move back in with my parents."

I nodded, sure that she was watching me in her peripheral vision, even if she was focused on the road. "Same. So, do you like teaching?"

Cara shrugged. "It's mostly fine. The testing requirements are ridiculous. The state uses a huge portion of our pathetically small budget to contract with this company to do these statewide standardized tests, and everyone agrees that it doesn't improve learning, only stresses out the kids, and basically wastes everyone's time."

"I wonder how much the testing company contributes to the governor's campaign."

"Plenty. Are you into politics?"

I shook my head. "I vote, and I even donate and write letters when there's an issue I'm passionate about. But I'm always torn between staying informed and staying mentally healthy, you know?"

"Definitely," Cara said. "I never watch cable news, and I try to focus on local elections so I don't feel so powerless. So yeah. I feel the same."

"Back to teaching…again. What do you like about it?"

"I get to make a bunch of high schoolers dissect frogs. That's always fun."

"Watching people vomit is fun?" I asked, shuddering at my own memories.

"They rarely vomit," she said, as though it was an absurd idea. "They mostly just complain. But there's a few who understand that it's a learning opportunity they haven't had before. I mean, provided they aren't filleting squirrels in their backyard."

"Ugh, gross."

"Yup."

"Want a drink?" I asked, and she nodded. We'd finally maneuvered the cooler into a position where we could open it from the front seat.

I pulled out two sparkling waters, cold from the ice refill at the hotel that morning, and handed her one. Cara believes in refilling jugs and reducing waste, but she also loves her bubbles.

"So," she went on, "those rare kids end up bent over the animal on their table, forgetting the formaldehyde stench, forgetting that their peers are watching, and exploring their world in a way a lot of them haven't done since they were little kids and gathering up handfuls of roly-polys."

I looked over at her, not wanting to miss the full import of what she was saying. I wanted to listen to her as well as she'd listened to me, and for the first time, I realized that our conversations weren't just killing time. At least, they weren't for me. I wanted to get to know Cara. I was enjoying getting to know her and realizing that she was someone worth knowing. Maybe I'd failed to notice that before, but I knew it now.

I also suspected that she didn't have an abundance of friends, that like me, she worked a lot and that most of her friendships had been couple friendships, tenuous relationships that probably wouldn't survive their divorce.

"That's a good reason to teach," I said, refocusing, "to give them that experience. Do you ever keep track of your old students?"

"Do I stalk them on social media, you mean?" she asked, glancing at me. "Totally. I found a few sad stories, but a few good ones. One Olympic athlete, a foster parent, a kid who invented some kind of special shoe? More than one in prison. Some of my favorite kids grew up and got science degrees of their own. It's nice to feel like I might've inspired that a little."

"You definitely did. Do you know why I ended up with an accounting major?"

"Hot professor?" she guessed.

I half turned in my seat to look at her. "How did you know?"

She laughed. "Are you serious?"

"Half serious." I grinned at the memories. Much better than frog dissection. "My parents had been going on and on for years about making sure that I had a plan after graduation. I always wanted to study music, but I didn't want to get a teaching certification, and jobs in music outside of teaching are rare. I didn't want to try for a record deal. I just…"

"You just wanted to enjoy music," Cara said. "I just wanted to look for bugs in the dirt. It's a shame that it's so hard to find a place in the world when you don't fit into the top one hundred careers."

"Exactly." I was a little startled that she'd understood so quickly. "So I tried a few different classes."

"And you had a hot accounting professor."

"And I had a hot accounting professor. And it was easy for me. I understand spreadsheets. And musical notation. It's everything else in the world that's difficult."

"Did you like being an accountant?" she asked.

I laughed. "Of course not. But I hated it less than most things, and that makes me luckier than most people. Plus, it paid well enough that I could save up for the store, and if it turns out…If it turns out that I can't keep the store open, it's a good backup plan."

Cara nodded slowly. "I hope you never need a backup plan."

I looked at her, surprised again. She kept doing that. "Thank you," I said. "What about you? Any secret aspirations for the future? Is there an opera singer or a bank executive or college professor hidden somewhere in there?" I pretended to try to peer inside her ear without distracting her driving too much.

It made me sad when she seemed to deflate a little, her thoughtful expression turning sad. "I want a lot of things," she said, "but none of them are career related."

And as hard as I pestered, miles of road passing underneath us, she wouldn't tell me a single one.

Chapter Thirteen

We reached Gila National Forest late that afternoon.

"*Hee-la*," said Cara. "Not *Gee-la*."

"Picky, picky, Coral."

"Nice try, Hiney, but I'm pretty sure I can win this game."

"I surrender," I said, laughing.

The drive through the forest was wonderful, especially after hours of desert with only the suggestion of mountains in the distance. Mature pine trees were dense walls on each side of the road. Neither Cara nor I spoke. We soaked in the deep green beauty. A wide river flowed through a break in the trees. I wanted to stop, but there was no shoulder to speak of, and anyway, we were almost to the visitors' center.

When we finally parked, Cara got out of the car and stretched, moaning. "Cars suck."

"If we'd flown, we would've been there two fucking days ago."

"*Nooo*," Cara said. "Don't say that."

"But," I said placatingly, "we would've missed all those amazing alien facts."

"We definitely should've flown."

We took a couple bottles of water, reusable bottles that Cara refilled at the hotel because she'd said that people who didn't care about the environment were basically shitting in their own living rooms. Not an image I'll ever be able to get out of my head.

Cara changed into her fancy hiking shoes. I wore my sneakers.

It was only about a half mile from the parking lot to the cliff dwellings, through well-marked trails edged in wildflowers and boulders.

I was sore enough from being in the car that the walk felt nice until it started to take us straight uphill. Before long, I was just leaning forward and hoping my feet would continue to prevent me falling on my face.

Cara walked behind me, becoming winded as she tried to explain the history of the site.

"The Mogollon people settled here about seven hundred"—pause for breath—"years ago, but eventually moved on. No one knows"—gasping for air—"why."

"You don't…have to be my tour guide," I managed.

"What? And waste…all those hours of research? That…would be silly."

"Fine. But wait…until you've caught…your breath."

"Is it the elev…elevation, or are we…really that out of shape?"

We didn't say much else. At one point, I heard Cara mutter, "Better be worth it," and I gave a gasping half laugh.

We got to the sign at the top and collapsed onto a bench. "I have to start exercising more," Cara said, then chugged her water bottle.

"Yeah. Right." I agreed with her, but it came out sarcastic. Really, if I hadn't started an exercise routine by my age, was it likely to happen? No. I'd made my peace with it.

Cara and I sat, looking around while we recovered.

I pointed at the metal railing, spray-painted yellow, along the stone stairs.

"The Mogollon people were clearly safety conscious."

Cara poured the last drop of her water bottle on my head. It felt wonderful.

When we finally made it back onto our feet, I couldn't believe what I saw. The houses looked like someone could've been living in there a few decades ago, not a few centuries. The stone walls were built into the cave with wooden crossbars and openings for windows.

"Forty-six rooms making up five dwellings, each of them—hmm." Cara peered at the sign. "Yes, each of them much bigger than my apartment."

"Are they serious? Can we just go inside?" I asked, staring at a ladder that led up into another set of rooms.

"They've been here seven hundred years. I imagine they'll survive us."

We climbed ladders, walked up stairs, and stood on smooth dirt floors, marveling at this place where the people who came before us had worked and loved and made music and lived their lives.

"Is it weird that I kind of miss them?" I whispered, trying to decipher the remains of a painted mural.

"I was just thinking the same thing," Cara said softly, coming to stand beside me. The back of her hand brushed mine. "I want to meet them and hear about…everything."

All of sudden, her hand was in mine. I didn't know which one of us had done it. Maybe both.

I didn't want to think about what it meant, but I also didn't want to move and mess it up. I looked at that mystery of a mural and reveled in the feeling of her soft fingers and the brush of her warm palm against mine.

How long had it been since I touched another person? Not my parents' quick hugs or slapping a paperback into Doug's hands, but something else, or at least, the prelude to something else.

Cara was different from the person I thought I knew. She was charming, hilarious, and fun. I was suddenly deeply grateful that she had decided we needed…*deserved*…to take this trip.

This trip away from our worries, from our stresses, from the catastrophe of our marriages.

I let my fingers slip out of her hand as I stepped away.

To Cara's credit, she didn't make an issue of it. We walked through the cliff dwellings twice, pointing out new facets of the homes, asking each other questions that neither of us had the answer to.

Eventually, Cara stopped and pulled out her phone. "Step behind the window," she said.

I walked around and looked through the opening at Cara's face behind her phone. She looked calm and happy.

I smiled and waved at the camera.

CHAPTER FOURTEEN

A few other tourists had arrived, and one of them looked at me and grinned when my stomach audibly grumbled. As huge as breakfast had been, it was a long time ago now. I hadn't checked the clock, but my stomach said it was dinnertime.

"Ready to go?" I asked Cara.

She took one last look around. "Yes. And never."

I led the way on the path to the parking lot, stopping halfway down a rocky slope.

"What's that?" I asked, pointing to an animal the size of a Labrador, snuffling ahead at the bottom of a boulder.

"How should I know?" Cara asked, standing on tiptoe and narrowing her eyes.

"You're the biologist."

Cara rolled her eyes. "Oh," she said, "that's a javelina."

"I knew you'd know. What's a javelina?"

"It's a distant relative of pigs. Very distant. Sort of a rodent-like pig."

"Giant hairy rat pig. Got it. I'll definitely be googling him later. Is he going to come at us with those tusks?" I asked.

As if it had heard me, it lifted its hairy snout in our direction.

"Um…" Cara said, taking a step backward.

The javelina grunted. It opened its mouth briefly to show not just the two bottom tusks, but two upper ones as well. They were long and yellow and sharp.

I stepped backward, too, my feet making a loud crunching sound on the gravel.

The javelina grunted again and charged, tiny hooves pounding the dirt, barreling toward us with surprising speed.

Cara and I ran back toward the cliff dwellings, panting as we tried to keep our footing on the rocky path, glancing behind us constantly as the tusks and the fast, panting grunts grew closer.

I was a little heavier than Cara, and I expected that she'd outpace me quickly, but I managed to keep up. I supposed that she wasn't going on a lot of long runs after teaching all day any more than I was closing up a music shop at midnight and hitting the gym.

Then Cara's foot slipped, and she hit one knee hard on the rocky ground.

I stopped. "Come on," I said gently, grabbing her arms and pulling her up as fast as I could without dislocating anything.

I swore I could feel the javelina's hot breath on my ankles as we ran.

Even without Cara's fall, I doubt we could've outrun the thing. We would've ended up tusk-gored and bitten and probably rabid, for all I know.

But maybe the little monster was just showing off, or maybe it knew we could escape inside the walls of the cliff dwelling. Maybe it got a whiff of our sweat and decided that we wouldn't be very tasty.

Whatever its thoughts, by the time we reached the outer wall, it had vanished. Only a few crushed bushes and a haze of kicked up dirt remained, and Cara and I could've caused that as easily as the javelina.

I looked carefully down the path, my eyes scanning the brush. There was no movement, not a sound.

But there was a fierce stink, the sort of eye-watering, gaggingly strong stench that was impossible to ignore.

"Fuck, are we being attacked by skunks, too?" I asked.

Cara gasped, then gagged, wiping sweat from her face as she limped to a bench. "I'd bet that's javelina musk. I'll look it up later."

"You have fun with that," I said, then started to laugh, wheezing a little because I was so completely winded. "Oh, thank God Badger isn't here. That thing would've eaten him whole."

Cara's mouth dropped open in an expression of horror.

"Don't worry," I said. "I'd never take him out in nature. He has zero survival skills. How is your knee?"

She stretched it out, examining the scraped skin. "Not too bad. Just a little bruised."

"Are you okay to walk back to the car?"

"As opposed to living in the cliff dwellings and eating cactus until it doesn't hurt anymore?"

"Yes, smart-ass. Or you could lean on me. Or if it's really bad, I can go find you crutches or some big strong paramedics."

Cara grinned. "Tempting, but I'm good to walk."

We waited until a bigger group of tourists was leaving and followed them, letting them flush out the wildlife for us.

We were exhausted and drained from the adrenaline rush when we finally pulled back onto the road.

Cara had poured clean water over her knee, insisting that it was her turn to drive. I pulled out drinks and snacks from the cooler for both of us, noting that Cara's supply of bagged, prepopped popcorn was already dwindling and wondering how I could still be hungry with javelina musk lingering in my nose.

As soon as my mouth was full, I started searching for appealing local restaurants. We were distressingly far from a city with a decent population.

"It looks like an hour and a half," I said.

Cara groaned. "I'm finally starting to miss home. There are probably two hundred restaurants within an hour and a half of my apartment."

"I could go buy ingredients from four different stores and cook a three-course meal in an hour and a half," I said.

"I could have Japanese appetizers, a Brazilian main course, and a French dessert in an hour and a half," Cara said.

"I could get a custom cake with my face on it and deliver slices of it to my ten closest friends, at each of their homes, in an hour and a half."

"I could make a replica of the Golden Gate Bridge with supermarket baguettes and then eat it—all—in an hour and a half."

We were ridiculous, but at least we entertained each other.

Cara pulled face wipes out of the glove compartment, offering me one after she saw me side-eyeing her cleansing ritual. She brushed her hair and applied lip gloss and looked very much like she hadn't been running for her life minutes before.

I took one look at myself in the mirror and decided I'd better try to do the same. There was something about that streak of purple that made me look either extremely cool or deranged, depending on how recently I'd brushed my hair. I braided each side into a thick braid, then held a bottle of water from the cooler against the back of my neck.

Finally, finally, we found a Mexican restaurant. There were even enough cars in the parking lot to give the impression that the food was edible.

"This is perfect," Cara said.

"Because they'll immediately bring us chips and salsa?"

"Exactly, Honey. Exactly."

In five minutes, we were seated at a table and had already placed our orders and were halfway through our first basket of tortilla chips.

"Not the best chips. Not the best salsa. And yet, somehow I don't mind," I said.

"It's the near-death experience. Being almost gored by wild animals always makes me hungry, too." Cara seemed to be trying to scoop more salsa than was possible onto her chip.

I gestured to it. "Does it make you try to break the laws of physics, too?"

"Always," she said, giving up and putting the chip in her mouth, then pouring a little salsa straight from the bowl into her mouth.

I laughed out loud. "I don't know if I can keep going places with you if you're going to embarrass me with your poor salsa etiquette."

Without expression, Cara poured the remaining chips onto a plate and placed the empty chip basket upside down on my head, like a hat.

"Ah…" the waiter said, setting down our margaritas. His nametag read *Fenske*.

I made eye contact with Fenske, peeking from under the chip basket. "May we have more chips, when you have a chance?"

"Sure," he said and walked away, shaking his head.

Cara was grinning widely. "It looks fantastic on you."

"Red is my color," I said, finally removing the basket and setting it back on the table.

The chips and salsa may have been mediocre, but the margaritas were delicious, and when our enchiladas came, they were impressive, both in size and quality.

"This place is a hidden gem," Cara said. "That's what my Yelp review is going to say."

"Oh, and our Mesmio review," I reminded her.

"Oops," she said, pulling out her phone and shooting a few seconds of video, including me drinking out of both our straws at once. Thankfully, she stopped recording before I dribbled margarita all over my shirt. She definitely wouldn't have edited it out for me. I had a giant smear of ketchup on my chin in an earlier video, and it was still out there for the world to see.

Once the worst of Cara's hunger was sated, she slowed down, watching me unabashedly lick grease off my fingers.

"Who was your first love?" she asked.

"This enchilada," I said with my mouth full. "Who was yours?"

Cara took a long drink of her margarita. "Well, I was in seventh grade."

"Oh, we're starting really early, then."

"Do you want to hear this or not? Her name was Melissa. She had these Elton John–style glasses."

I laughed. "Oh my God. Was this the eighties?"

"Shut up. She also had a notebook that was covered, I mean absolutely covered, in Lisa Frank stickers."

"Hot."

Cara rolled her eyes and took another bite. After a minute, she said, "I followed her around like she was the Messiah for two years."

"That's a long time, at that age."

"Did I mention she played guitar?"

I laughed so hard that I choked. "Oh no," I said, when I could manage to speak. "Were you a groupie?"

Cara shrugged, piling a bit each of enchilada, refried beans, and Spanish rice onto a spoon. "Can you be a groupie for a twelve-year-old who only knows two songs?" She dipped her entire spoon in salsa before eating it. She might be a genius.

"Depends. Was one of them 'Knockin' on Heaven's Door'?"

Cara's mouth fell open. "How on earth could you know that?"

"It's a classic beginner song. So you were obsessed with a musician. Happens to the best of us. What happened next?"

Cara gave a one-shoulder shrug. "I tried to learn guitar, but I gave up pretty quickly."

"Right. The elbows."

She laughed. "It's weird how you remember the random things that come out of my mouth. Yes, the elbows. Where are they supposed to go? What is their role?"

I shook my head at her. "So no guitar. What happened then?"

"Oh, eventually we went to high school, and by then, I had a crush on someone new every week."

"Poor Melissa."

"She never liked me back. She dated a baseball player all through high school. I lost track of her after that."

"She's not on Facebook?" I asked.

"No, and I hate how weird I find that," Cara said, grinning. "How can you be our age and not at least have a profile with a picture that's ten years out of date?"

"That is mysterious," I agreed.

"What about you, Honey?"

"I am not mysterious. I post crap constantly. If there's a video out there of someone throwing cheese slices on a baby's head, I've reposted it."

Cara just stared at me.

I sighed. "I'm afraid I was a late bloomer. I was nineteen, and it was a woman I worked with at Subway."

"No one at all before that?"

"Passing infatuations, mostly with celebrities and book characters. But then there was Tamara."

"Pretty name."

"Beautiful woman. I mean, the kind that could stop traffic, except…"

"Except?" Cara prompted.

"She liked to drink vodka and blue Kool-Aid."

"So what?" Cara asked, amused.

"I mean, that's all she drank. All day. She kept a thermos with her at the register and refilled it during her lunch break. She'd already had her license suspended, so she rode home with whoever could take her."

Cara listened, wide-eyed.

"So, one night, that was me, and she was completely hammered by closing. She passed out in the passenger seat of my car, and I couldn't get her to wake up long enough to tell me her address."

"Dear goodness. What did you do?"

"What could I do?" I shook my head, pushing the last of the rice onto my spoon. "I took her home, to my house, to my parents' house, I mean."

Cara stared for a second, then laughed out loud. "What did your parents do?"

"My dad threw Tamara over his shoulder and carried her like a firefighter. My mom got her water and aspirin and got her tucked into bed. In my head, I was like, this is the beginning for us. She's going to wake up, be so grateful that I took care of her, and love me forever."

"Don't tell me. It didn't happen that way."

"She snuck out in the middle of the night, and I never saw her again."

"Wow," Cara said.

"Her tongue was always blue," I said a little wistfully.

"What's Tamara doing now? Do you know?"

"Oh, she's in prison."

"You're kidding," Cara said, in a tone that said she hoped I wasn't.

"Nope. She violated the Endangered Species Act."

Cara leaned forward. The waiter passed by, smiled at us, and kept going.

"She was caught with a baby sea turtle during Mardi Gras," I said.

Cara put both her hands over her mouth. "What?"

"Well, first she was arrested for public urination, then the officer saw that her pocket was moving. And dripping. That's where he found the sea turtle."

"You are making this up," Cara said, dropping her hands.

"No, if I was making up a story, it would be believable. So the turtle is fine. It goes to a rehabilitation center. But Tamara goes to prison."

"For turtle smuggling?"

"Well, for that and for punching a cop in the testicles for stealing her pet. She testified that it was a rare species of cat, then called the judge a stupid fuckface for not believing her. And then she vomited a bright blue substance, according to the news, all over her lawyer."

Cara tried hard not to laugh, but she managed to say, "I don't believe a word of this."

But I expected that response, and I already had my phone out.

I turned it to show her the article: "Houston Woman Convicted on Multiple Counts, Including Endangered Species Act Violation."

There's a picture, too. Tamara, still lovely, with a bright blue smile.

We finished the last bites of our meals and ordered dessert, chatting about our one-sided romances and cocktails that did not contain blue Kool-Aid.

"What about your first kiss?" Cara asked.

"Oh, it was magical. Freddie what's-his-name. Sixth grade. On the school bus on our way back from a field trip to a drastically boring cave."

"Hey, caverns can be cool."

"Nerd. Anyway, we were holding hands, and he leaned over to kiss me just as the bus hit a pothole. He slammed his face into mine so hard that I broke a tooth."

Cara shook her head, staring at me in horror. "That's traumatizing. Is that why you only kiss women now?"

"Yes. That's why I only kiss women now. Obviously." I laughed. "What about you?"

"Oh, mine was much better. I was in fourth grade, and a boy on the playground kissed me…with tongue."

"No," I said, not sure whether to laugh, but Cara was grinning.

"Yes, except I didn't know about French kissing, so I kept my lips together, and he just licked my mouth."

I had to laugh, and Cara just shook her head at me.

"Gross," I said. "But that doesn't count. What's the first kiss you actually participated in?"

"Oh," Cara mocked. "Your dental injury counts, but me being lapped at like a dog doesn't? Fine. It was five long, kissless years later."

I tried to count with margarita-brain. It took me a minute. "High school?"

"Yes. No, the summer before high school. This is how I got over Melissa and her seductive guitar. My parents had some friends visiting, and their son—"

"Friends, right? Not family members?"

Cara looked even more grossed out than when she told me about the licking kiss. "Not family, you weirdo. No, friends from Mexico who were in New Orleans for vacation. Their son was a year older than me, with these big brown eyes and unkempt hair. I adored him immediately."

"Did he play guitar?" I smirked.

"No." She paused. "Piano."

I smirked harder.

"Anyway," she said, ignoring me. "He was hot, and he had this soft way of speaking, and I'd been listening to a lot of Enrique Iglesias. Honestly, it was entirely predictable. I don't know what my parents were thinking."

"What do you mean?"

"Inviting an attractive teenage boy to stay for a week at a house with a...*willing* teenage girl?"

"You mean *horny*."

Cara glared. "Passionate," she said, then sighed as though giving in to my vocabulary. "Honestly, within two hours, we were making out behind the shed, and he snuck into my bedroom every single night. It's a miracle I wasn't pregnant after that week."

"Wait," I said. She had my complete attention, even though the waiter had arrived with cake. "Are you telling me that you had your first real kiss the same day you had sex for the first time?"

Fenske discreetly set down the plates and walked away.

"No," Cara said. "We just kissed for the first two nights."

"Cara, that's still really fast. And you were what, fourteen?"

"Almost."

I stared at her.

"What?" She was looking back at me, wide-eyed with confusion. "It was consensual."

"Isn't there some kind of age you have to be before you *can* consent? I don't know what it is, but it's not thirteen. You were just a baby."

I sounded angry, but Cara seemed to understand that I wasn't angry at her. She put a hand on my arm, and I tried to relax so she didn't feel how tense my muscles were.

"I was fine," she said gently. "I *am* fine. Yes, I was probably too young, but he was gentle and nice. We talked on the phone for years after that. He would tell me about school and his basketball team. I would tell him about having a different crush every week and about how desperate I was to get out of New Orleans and go to college somewhere new and exciting."

I made my foot stop violently tapping. It was shaking the whole table.

"He's a creep," I said, "and I'll hate him forever."

Cara nodded. "I'm okay with that." Then she opened my hand and put a fork into it.

The waiter had brought two enormous slices, cheesecake and chocolate cake, and Cara and I split them both, making noises that approached the erotic.

"This feels like the wrong thing. Shouldn't we be getting makeovers or something?" Cara said, licking chocolate off her top lip.

"Uh…what?"

"That's what you usually do to show your ex that you're over them, right? You get a haircut, join a gym, start dating someone younger."

"I don't want to do any of those things," I said.

"Neither do I. I also don't think it would work. I got a haircut and joined a gym last year, and Lorenzo never noticed."

I noted that. Either Cara's gym days didn't include running or she'd kept pace with me instead of leaving me behind while the rabid javelina was chasing us.

Cara the passionate teenager. Cara the compassionate adult. I was learning new things about her every day.

"By Christmas," Cara was saying, "there were days I didn't even see him. He'd be gone when I got up for work, and I'd be asleep before he got back. It was only dirty clothes in the hamper that showed he'd come home at all."

"You should've started dating someone younger. I bet he would've noticed that."

"Would he? I don't know." Cara picked up a stray piece of chocolate frosting and popped it into her mouth. "Anyway, I never wanted to have to go searching for romance, you know? All those matchmaking apps and programs seem so hard, especially after all these years without practice. I don't even know if I want to fall in love again. I don't know if it's worth the trouble."

I nodded. "All that getting-to-know-you, getting comfortable stuff is the worst. I want to be settled. I don't want to have to ask the questions and have the doubts. Maybe that's part of the problem, though. I didn't ask the questions. Maybe I shouldn't have assumed that she still meant what she said when we first got together. Or maybe I should've paid more attention when she said she had doubts. I thought we were fine because neither of us was getting arrested for turtle trafficking, but that's a pretty low bar. Maybe she grew into another person, and I didn't keep getting to know her."

Cara was watching me, fork hovering above her plate.

"What?"

"That's a lot of introspection. Here, have another margarita."

I laughed and accepted. She gave a smile and a polite wave to get Fenske's attention.

"I need you to get one thing straight, Honey," she said as he approached. "None of this is your fault. You don't take the blame for a cheater."

She ordered us both a second margarita, and I took my empty glass and touched it to hers.

"Same."

"Yes," she said. "Same. I spent weeks doing that, wondering what I could've done, what I could've been, that would've made Lorenzo be faithful to me. But the fact is, I was me, just like when I was a kid and in love with the guitarist with Elton John glasses. And I'm going to keep being me, and if that's not what they want…if that's not what *he* wants, then I'm glad he left."

She said it without quavering, but her eyes were wet. I placed my hand palm up on the table between us, and she took it, squeezing. I didn't feel the heart-pounding awareness that had accompanied holding her hand in the cliff dwellings, but this was, in its own way, no less intimate.

For the hundredth time, I wondered how I'd spent so much time with this woman over the years without getting to know her.

"At this point," I said, squeezing her hand tightly, "I'm pretty sure that no man deserves you."

"I don't know what that means coming from a lesbian."

I was still laughing when our second round of margaritas arrived.

Chapter Fifteen

I should've guessed that our hotel was nearby. Cara wasn't the type to drink two margaritas and get back on the road. But I didn't realize it was literally next door.

"I actually thought it was the one across the street," Cara said, checking our reservation. "But that's good. This one looks nicer."

We checked in, took the elevator to the third floor, found our room, each crawled into one of the two double beds, and switched off the lights.

Thirty seconds later, the edges of sleep within reach, Cara said, "What do you think is the key to a happy and lasting relationship?"

I groaned, too tired from talking and more than ready for sleep. "Is this from your road trip conversations list?"

"Come on," she said in such a chipper and cajoling tone that I had to wonder if my alcohol was burning off faster than hers.

"Money," I said, then paused to yawn. "Lots of sex. Not cheating on your wife with ugly-ass dudes."

She sat up. "You think Lorenzo is ugly? I mean, *he's* no Enrique Iglesias, but…"

"I think he could be a dreamboat if he ate more vegetables and got some plastic surgery."

But it wasn't true. He could get all the plastic surgery in the world, and he would still be the ogre who cheated on Cara. He would be ugly forever.

I yawned again. "Can I sleep now?"

Cara was silent for another thirty seconds. Then, "Did you see the new Mesmio reel?"

For several seconds, my margarita-soaked brain thought she was talking about our Mesmio. But then the pieces of our conversation clicked.

"No," I said, sounding more awake even to myself.

There was a rustling sound as Cara moved out of her bed and a tilting sensation as she crawled into mine. Then her phone screen lit up with enough lumens to scar my corneas.

"Ow," I said, closing my eyes.

She tapped, and after a moment, I heard Bridget's voice.

It felt like years since I'd heard her. Often, even when I was rewatching the same video over and over, I muted it for privacy. Or out of shame.

But there she was, speaking, her voice as familiar as my own. It nudged something in me that I thought she'd killed. I actually missed her, just for those first seconds.

"*We made some new friends onboard. This is Shea and Darren.*"

Shea was a tall white woman with a gentle smile. She was probably fifty years old, but something about her and Darren's matching red Hawaiian shirts made her seem older. Darren was Black, probably around the same age, and almost as tall. He smiled at the camera, too.

"They've been married for twenty years. Can you believe that? We were so happy to get to be a part of their anniversary celebration. Do you have any tips for us? Any secrets to a long and happy life together?"

She leaned close to Shea without moving her own face even slightly offscreen.

Shea had a calm voice. I imagined she'd rather be doing literally anything else on her anniversary than being interviewed by random strangers, but maybe I was projecting. She certainly didn't seem annoyed.

"*All the usual stuff,*" she said, "*communicate, make time for each other, make an effort to do little acts of thoughtfulness...and the dishes.*" She laughed. "*And don't think that just because you're committed you can be less polite. This person might be living with you for the rest of your life. Say please and thank you. Ask them about their day. Close the door when you poop.*"

Beside her, Darren burst out laughing. "*Good advice,*" he said, with a slight accent. Maybe Jamaican?

"*Do you have any advice of your own?*" Bridget asked. She seemed a little taken aback by Shea's advice. Maybe she was wondering when she'd last said please. I certainly couldn't remember.

Darren shook his head, but he said, "*Coffee and plants.*"

"*My two favorite things,*" Shea explained. "*I can't count how many times I've woken up to a fresh cup of coffee beside the bed or come home from work to find a new plant waiting for me. Hundreds. Maybe thousands.*"

"*Plus a new toy occasionally.*" Darren winked.

Shea covered her grin, and Bridget's face went slightly pink.

Oh, *toys*.

Then Shea launched into a description of her current favorite toy. I caught the words *suction* and *speed settings* before Bridget yanked the phone back toward her own face and started walking away.

"*Just another beautiful day in Cozumel,*" she said, her voice high and squeaky.

When the reel looped back to the beginning, Cara turned off her screen. We lay there in the dark, in the quiet.

I understood why Cara had shown this to me. It wasn't to be mean, which was my first assumption. Maybe it was, in part, a confirmation that Bridget and Lorenzo were doing more than escaping Cara and me. They were thinking about the future, planning it together.

But mostly, I think she wanted me to see Shea and Darren, happy after all their years together. Maybe Cara didn't have people like that, like my parents, to make her believe that love was more than the thing that happened in between heartbreaks.

"Hey," I said, turning toward her.

Cara snored in my face.

I laughed quietly, took the phone from her hands and plugged it in to charge, and lay back down, too tired to move to the other bed or to care when Cara threw one leg over both of mine and murmured something about climate change.

I patted her hand. "It's just a nightmare," I whispered. "The oil industry is dead and all the trash has been recycled." I paused, remembering. "And Melissa with the Elton John glasses really did like you back."

Cara smiled in her sleep.

Chapter Sixteen

It's Grand Canyon day!" Cara announced.

I half opened an eye, just enough to see the bedside clock. It was eight a.m., much later than I'd intended to sleep. I pulled the comforter over my head, but not before noticing that she was already fully dressed.

"Come on, sleepyhead," Cara said, bouncing on the foot of my bed.

"Do you have a reverse hangover?" I asked, trying to kick her through the comforter and mostly failing.

There was an ominous pause, and then Cara was talking in a different tone. I poked my head out, and her phone was right in my face. I screamed and retreated.

"The rare and glorious Honey only emerges briefly before coffee can be obtained. Did you catch that sound? She may be warning others of her species that there is danger approaching, or she may be producing a mating call. Let's see if we can determine which."

My comforter disappeared, yanked away by a traitor.

I growled, coming to all fours and launching myself at Cara, who shrieked, laughed, and dropped her phone under the bed.

She was still laughing as she wiggled herself halfway under the bed to retrieve it.

"You make me act ridiculous," Cara said.

"Me? Oh no. I'm not taking responsibility for your behavior." I grabbed my phone and said, "Hey, Siri. Search how to tolerate happy people when you have a hangover."

I dressed and repacked the little that I'd emptied from my suitcase, then called to check in with Florence while Cara finished arranging her curls. She paused to raise her pant leg and put a new bandage on her scraped knee.

Her capri pants had lace on the back pockets and small, embroidered flowers. I realized I was staring with my phone in my hand and turned away quickly.

"Honey!" Florence answered, her voice full of cheer. "Those hand-painted ukuleles came in, and we've already sold three!"

"What?" I couldn't remember the last time we'd sold three…of anything.

"Doug stood outside strumming one half the morning. Can't carry a tune in a bucket with a lid on, but it worked."

Doug definitely had a good ukulele vibe, chill and obviously talented, except for his singing voice. I could hear him faintly in the background, playing "Hakuna Matata."

It wasn't exactly on key, but it was fully enthusiastic. A few tiny voices joined in.

"I miss you guys," I said.

"Stop it. You're supposed to be having fun. Where are you? What was yesterday's stop?"

I told her about the cliff dwellings, downgrading our javelina experience to a sighting, and ended with, "Today, we'll be at the Grand Canyon, but not before dark if we don't hurry."

I made eye contact with Cara in the mirror.

"I'll let you get to it," said Florence.

We gathered everything and left the room. The plan was to load the car, grab a quick continental breakfast, and get on the road so we would have the whole afternoon for the Grand Canyon.

I paused only long enough to download a dozen Enrique Iglesias songs, which I planned to play when it was Cara's turn to drive, so I could look at the lyrics and sing along.

I followed Cara into the elevator, a bag hanging from each shoulder, and pushed the button for the lobby.

The elevator doors closed.

And all the lights went out.

For a full minute, Cara and I stood there, staring at the elevator doors, expecting them to open, the lights to turn back on, or for something, anything, to happen.

Nothing did.

"It seems that we are stuck in an elevator," I said, turning to where I knew Cara must be standing.

"Aren't there supposed to be emergency lights?" Cara whispered. It was cave dark, blackout dark. I couldn't remember any other time in my life when I had strained my eyes so hard and got nothing in return, not a flicker, not an outline, nothing.

"I'll ask the firefighters when they get here. You're not claustrophobic, are you?"

"No. You?"

"No. I'm hungry, though."

Cara laughed quietly. "I'm so sorry that we got trapped in an elevator before breakfast."

"Even before coffee," I moaned. "Though I'm grateful for an empty bladder."

"Oh no," Cara said. "Don't even say *bladder*. We should try to call someone."

"Do cell phones work in elevators?" I asked, but I was already pulling mine out of my pocket.

The light of the display was startlingly bright, as it had been last night, and a second later, Cara's joined mine.

We looked at each other in the eerie glow, then looked down and both started tapping.

"Nope," she answered a few seconds later. "Cell phones don't work in elevators."

"Super," I said. "But it's a hotel. It's not like they're not going to notice that an elevator isn't working."

"On a Monday morning?"

I turned my phone toward the elevator buttons. "Emergency!" I said, pushing it excitedly. Nothing happened.

I pushed it seventy more times with the same effect.

That was the moment when it stopped being a funny mishap.

I pounded on the door and shouted for help until my fist hurt and my voice was hoarse. I had this image of someone opening the elevator doors to find me and Cara, dehydrated and wide-eyed, covered in cave dirt for some reason, reverting to grunts because we'd lost our ability to understand human language.

It was absurd. I knew that, even as my hands hit the door, but I didn't want to paint a realistic picture. I didn't want to think of the realities of being in here for five more minutes, let alone how many hours it would take before someone rescued us.

When I gave up, winded, heart pounding, I turned around and leaned against the closed doors, letting myself slide to the floor.

I had a sudden, vibrant memory of the night before my wedding, sliding down to the thick rug in the bedroom Bridget and I shared. It was our first apartment, an absolute shithole. The heater didn't work. The dishwasher door had to be braced closed with a broomstick or it wouldn't run. Every single windowpane had a crack.

But at twenty-five, it was the most we could afford and still get takeout once a week.

Bridget had a thick white rug that I always said looked like someone had skinned a yeti. That's where I was standing, the night before our wedding, when she told me that she wasn't sure she could go through with it.

I don't think it was a sign or a premonition. I don't even think the feeling stayed with her long. In any case, at ten the next morning, I was sliding a ring onto her finger, and she was laughing through tears as she fumbled to find my ring in the pocket of her voluminous tulle dress.

But that moment in our room—with her confessing her doubts and worries about what married life would be for us, whether we were too young to make a commitment, whether we would resent each other or feel trapped after a few years, whether having an official, legally wedded wife would impede her career in an industry dominated by middle-aged straight men in Texas—that moment I slid to the floor and put my hands in the yeti fur rug and wanted nothing in the world more than to share that shitty apartment with Bridget for the rest of my life.

My life. My life now would've been unimaginable to twenty-five-year-old Honey. Even aside from being trapped in an elevator, it would've been a nightmare to me then.

Maybe what was really unimaginable is how much I would change in the next fourteen years.

Cara sat beside me, getting herself situated and untangled from her bags before turning her phone display off. I did the same. It made sense, conserving the battery, though I couldn't have said what we were conserving it for.

I listened, my eyes closed in the dark, but I couldn't hear anything except my breathing and an occasional shifting movement from Cara.

She found my hand and held it. It was starting to be a daily thing with us, enough that it was beginning to feel natural. I gripped her hand hard and didn't let go.

Neither of us wore our wedding rings. I'd taken mine off almost as soon as Bridget walked out the door, even though it was my favorite ridiculous tradition. I didn't care that we'd spent five years paying them off. It was a row of sapphires in white gold, and it was the most beautiful thing I'd ever owned.

"I'm sorry," I said to Cara now, feeling her soft fingers move comfortingly against the back of my hand.

"I've been told that it's okay to have emotions."

"Huh. Really?"

"That's the rumor. I think I have granola bars."

"I saw those. They're hard as bricks, and I'm not that desperate yet," I said. I could hear the faint rasp in my voice from the screaming. "You know what I want?"

"Coffee?"

"And tiramisu."

"Interesting breakfast choice," Cara said. "I think I'd prefer French toast at this hour."

"Powdered sugar?"

"Nope. Syrup. The real stuff, straight from the tree."

"I'm pretty sure there's a process before—"

"Nope," Cara said. "Drill it, tap it, pour it on my plate."

I laughed, even though I wasn't feeling amused. But the action of laughing did calm me a little, and I managed a deep breath.

Now that my eyes had adjusted, I could see faint light in the edges of the door. I took that as a sign that we wouldn't suffocate, at least.

"Did you know," Cara said, "that the rivers that created the Grand Canyon have revealed nearly two billion years of the Earth's geologic history?"

"You really do find joy in teaching me things, don't you?"

"I really like to share things that I find amazing."

I nodded, though she couldn't see me. "That *is* amazing. Are there javelinas at the Grand Canyon?"

"Definitely not."

"Are you lying to make me feel better?"

"Yes. Also, there are giant hairy scorpions, but we probably won't see any."

I closed my eyes again. "I feel pretty confident in my ability to outrun a scorpion."

"Only if you see it coming," Cara said. "I mean, yes, good point, no need to worry about scorpions."

"You are a horrible person to be stuck with in an elevator," I said.

There was a long, quiet moment. I almost thought I was going to have to apologize, but when Cara spoke, her voice was calm and thoughtful.

"If I'm going to be stuck in an elevator with someone," Cara said, "I'd rather it be you than almost anyone I know."

"Really? Why?" I was still a little embarrassed about screaming and hitting the door. I worried it had come off more as a tantrum than an attempt to get help.

"Do you remember, a year or so ago, when…when Bridget was in that car accident?"

Of course, I remembered. I was at Cara and Lorenzo's apartment, awkwardly waiting for Bridget to show up. She was late, and I was irritated because that meant I was the one who had to pretend to have social skills while our hosts were finishing one of the too-elaborate meals they always made when they invited us.

So when my phone vibrated, I answered, thinking I could show Bridget my irritation without Cara or Lorenzo noticing. I had the words and the tone ready.

But when I put the phone to my ear, I heard Bridget crying so hard she couldn't speak.

On the floor of the elevator, I felt Cara move and imagined her leaning her head back against the wall. "You said, 'Whatever happened, I love you and I'm here for you. But you have to tell me right now because I can't stand hearing you cry without knowing if you're okay.'"

"That's a lot of words when what I really meant was *Pull your shit together and talk to me.*"

"It's not, though," Cara said. "You said exactly what you meant, and when Bridget said she'd been in an accident, you left without saying a word to us. To Lorenzo or me. We didn't know what happened for days."

I sat up straight. “Oh no, Cara. I’m so sorry.”

“No,” she said, nudging my foot with hers. “That’s not the point I’m making. The point is that there wasn’t room for anyone but her, when she needed you. And that’s amazing. Do you know what Lorenzo said when my father died?”

I nudged her foot in answer.

“He said, ‘I guess that’s one less stop we have to make at Christmas.’ ”

“What? No way. I mean, I know he’s sleeping with my wife, but I didn’t know he was that big an asshole.”

Thankfully, Cara laughed at that. She said, “I told you that I didn’t have a good relationship with my father, but that wasn’t what I needed from my husband after news of his death. What I needed was *Whatever happens, I love you and I’m here for you.* Nothing too hard. Nothing too complicated. Sometimes…sometimes I’d wonder, what if I’d married my Enrique Iglesias, what would he say? What would he do? But that’s not fair. He could’ve grown up to be a complete asshole, too.”

I listened and thought about what she said, but while I thought, I finally let go of Cara’s hand while I felt around for the latches on my guitar case. I opened the lid and pulled it onto my lap, strumming at a whisper.

She went on, “So when all the mess with Lorenzo and Bridget came out, part of me thought how disappointed she’s about to be, after having been loved the way a person should be loved, for such a long time.”

“Our marriage wasn’t all like that,” I protested. “I said some snide shit too over the years.”

“Oh, that doesn’t surprise me at all.”

I kicked her and heard her snicker.

“But the point is,” she went on, “Bridget had those lovely moments as, I don’t know, as points of comparison. When you said snide shit, when you said true and wonderful things to her, she got to pick which to believe.”

“But from Lorenzo, you only got the snide shit. And the hurtful shit.”

“And not much else,” Cara agreed.

I took a deep breath of the stale air. “So what does that have to do with us being stuck in an elevator?” I asked.

"Honey," she said, and there was softness in her voice that I hadn't heard before.

Before I could wonder about it, the elevator jolted, taking my breath away.

We were definitely going to die. I reached out for Cara's hand and only found it because she was reaching for me, too. We held on tight.

Then the lights flickered and stayed on.

Cara and I gasped, and I stood, pulling her up with me. I reached over and immediately started pushing the *door open* button repeatedly.

And it did.

Cara let out a sigh of relief, and I honest-to-God cheered. I put my foot out to hold the door while I returned my guitar to its case, and we gathered our bags, throwing straps over our shoulders and shoving phones back in pockets. Cara stood between the open doors like she'd be willing to let them crush her rather than leaving me to be stuck inside again.

I gave her a quick hug in the elevator doorway before we stepped into the hallway and into our freedom.

We stopped, looking left and right at the long hallway of closed doors. We were still on the third floor.

We wheeled our suitcases down the stairs.

Chapter Seventeen

"I can't believe that was only an hour," I said as we hurried to the car.

"Didn't you say something about time portals to that guy in Roswell?" Cara asked.

"Uh, time dilation? Wouldn't make a difference unless that elevator was very, very fast."

We were skipping continental breakfast in favor of drive-through breakfast burritos. We debated our coffee situation while waiting in line.

"The coffee might be good here," Cara said with considerable doubt.

"It's possible that there's a real coffee shop somewhere ahead."

"A real coffee shop. With no line."

"Right," I agreed. "Because it's a weekday."

"It's worth the risk."

It wasn't worth the risk.

Four hours later, we stopped at a convenience store for very large cups of drip coffee and bottled iced coffee for the cooler, just in case the drip was undrinkable, which it absolutely was.

Another hour down the road and happily caffeinated, Cara turned down Billie Eilish and shifted sideways in the passenger seat to face me.

"So, were you a practicing accountant before you opened Strings & Things?"

"For a while," I said, mentally apologizing to Billie Eilish for the interruption. "Then I taught guitar lessons. Then I did both."

"And then Bridget was promoted."

"Yes. Then Bridget was a VP, and all the money I'd been saving to open the shop felt like pennies. She was always…Keep in mind that she is still the most despicable person alive."

"How could I forget?" Cara asked, but she was smiling slightly.

"Just such an easy person to hate with all your soul. But she was always more concerned about people than money. I will give her that."

Cara nodded. "I believe that. Lorenzo told me that she used to buy snacks and shampoo and stuff for kids in her dorm that didn't have much extra money."

"Right. She grew up solidly middle class, but you'd never know it. Did you know she paid for my guitar tattoo? I'd been wanting it for years, and we couldn't really afford it. But she used her first Christmas bonus to do that for me, even after I told her that we should save it. Or spend it on something she wanted. So, yeah. It wasn't a big surprise when she told me that we had the money for the storefront, and that we should just do it. Just rent the place, start fixing it up, filling it up with merchandise. I thought she was joking at first. I thought we were years out from being able to do that. But we started spending all our free time getting our business proposal ready, planning our inventory, fighting over the name."

"Let me guess," Cara said. "Strings & Things wasn't your choice."

I glanced over. Cara had her bottled caramel coffee in her hands, rotating it slowly. I wondered if she missed her fancy cups and porcelain sugar bowl and creamer pitcher. The coffee she'd poured for me at her house was far better than this.

"No," I said. "I wanted a shop name that was…"

"Cooler?"

"I guess," I said. "Though some people have asked if we named it after the TV show *Stranger Things*."

"That makes it slightly cooler?"

"Slightly. Bridget said that the names *I* picked were off-putting, that they would attract one kind of buyer, and that we needed more than that to stay afloat."

"And did you? Stay afloat?"

"Nope," I said. "I had to quit my accounting job as soon as we opened. We wouldn't have survived if Bridget had wanted to do the same. She paid for everything. The house, the bills, the groceries. The store breaks even if I don't take a paycheck."

"Oh, Honey. I had no idea."

I shrugged, twirling my purple hair around my fingers with one hand on the wheel. "We have enough money. We…*had.* I'm too scared to think about what's going to happen when all this is official. To the shop, I mean. And to Florence and Doug."

I didn't remind her that I meant it literally, that I hadn't had the guts to open the envelope, as though I could just keep delaying my failure, the end of my dream.

I don't know when Cara started recording me, but when she showed me later, I agreed to let her post it. I wasn't above a pity sale or two.

Florence and Doug would be okay. I'd make sure of it. I'd tell them to start looking for new jobs the minute I got home. They deserved to have time to find something they wanted, and if the store held on for a few more months, then I'd take what time I had.

I'd have to start working on my résumé, too, I realized. It was long out of date. Maybe I wouldn't have to go back to accounting right away. Maybe I could find a job at stupid Guitar Center. Maybe I'd go back to school and…do what? It wasn't as though I wanted a career change. I was doing what I wanted to do. I just wasn't succeeding.

Cara was still talking, and I answered her absently. I'd done such a good job of setting aside my worries and enjoying this trip. I had a talent for denial. But at some point, I was going to have to form a real plan.

Eventually, Cara gave up on trying to get my attention, and we listened to my playlist, interrupted now and then by Sir David Attenborough telling us to "*keep right.*"

Chapter Eighteen

We reached the Grand Canyon by midafternoon. We passed the East Entrance, the parking lot so full that dozens of cars were idling, waiting for even a chance to park.

"There are other lookouts, right?" I asked. "I don't care about the gift shop and all that, do you?"

"No. Let's just drive awhile and see if there's a place to pull over."

There were several places to pull over, all of them packed.

Cara stared out the window. "I guess we're not the only ones on spring break after all."

"Honestly, the view from here is so amazing. I almost don't care," I said, even though I was the one driving.

Layers of orange and red and brown stretched down and away from us, feeling endless.

The road seemed to lead away from the canyon for miles, but just when I was about to suggest we reroute, the trees ended, and our view of the canyon opened up again, even more vast and lovely.

There wasn't a real parking lot here, only a gravel space with enough room for Cara's car, but there was no one else around, and we didn't dare miss our chance. I pulled over, and we both clambered out of the car and as close to the edge of the canyon as we dared. There were no railings here, nothing but the two of us and this natural wonder laid out before us.

"Honestly, I just expected a big hole," I said.

Cara laughed, and I could hear it faintly echoing off the ancient walls.

We recorded our reels and took pictures for Cara to add to the

Mesmio she'd made for us. We pretended to skip rocks over the canyon and shouted stupid words to hear the echo. I convinced Cara to sit next to me with our feet hanging over the edge.

"Just look," I told her, when she seemed too tense to notice anything but her own fear. "Here we are, and all of that, all of those ancient rocks, all that history, is right under our feet." I wiggled mine, and she looked out with me, past our toes to what felt like the entire world, certainly more of it than we'd ever seen. Miles upon miles. Eons upon eons.

"Hey," Cara said, pointing.

I squinted to see. There were people riding horses along a trail in the distance.

"Next time," I joked.

Shadows of clouds crossed below, moving like ripples over the uneven rock formations.

It was quiet except for the wind, and the rocks gave off a fresh, somehow warm smell.

"Thank you for coming with me," Cara said.

We'd moved back from the edge now and sat cross-legged on a large slab of rock free of the spindly bushes gripping the few places where soil remained.

"I know you had your own reasons for wanting to get away," she went on, and I thought about the unopened envelope on my desk again, feeling the twinge of anxiousness that never seemed to go away.

Cara pulled me back out of my thoughts, back to the majesty of what lay out before us.

"But I am grateful. I don't think I would've gone alone."

"Why not?" I looked at her, beautiful dark hair whipping around in the breeze.

"I don't think that I ever learned how to do things alone. How to *be* alone. I relationship-hopped through college, and by the time I graduated, I was with Lorenzo. I lived with college roommates, then with him, and this is the first time I've ever been by myself long enough to rearrange the furniture." She huffed a laugh. "And then I immediately came to see if you would go with me, so I didn't have to stay alone in my apartment or go alone on the road. I just couldn't take nine days with my own thoughts. How pathetic is that?"

I wanted to hug her, but I settled for poking her in the cheek.

"Ow," she protested.

"So you haven't been alone because you've always had people around who love you? That's not pathetic. That's sort of ideal human existence. Sure, rearrange your furniture. Sure, make time for what you want. But the goal of all this isn't some mythical independence. Didn't you ever read that dude who said no man is an island? Tolstoy?"

"John Donne."

"Right. I mean, romance isn't the goal. Or sex. I know you're a biologist, but sex isn't the whole point. I mean, it's pretty good. Really good. Great, sometimes. But it can't be the whole point."

"So what is?"

"It's us." I hurried to add, "It's all of us. Friendships and family and community and all that crap. And joy and wonder. It's sitting in front of the Grand Canyon and actually thinking about who we are and what we want."

Cara stared at me. "That's pretty deep, Honeybee."

"I'd be perfectly happy if you never called me that again," I said, and she laughed.

"So, what do you want, *Honey*?"

I shrugged. "I got what I wanted. I wanted a music shop and a wife and to not have to worry too much about the electric bill."

"Is that still what you want?"

I stretched out my legs onto the warm rock and leaned over to dust off my guitar tattoo. "Three months ago, I would've said yes without hesitation. It's everything that I worked for, and I was happy. But now I have to wonder, was I? Am I? Because all of a sudden there's this great gaping hole." I gestured to the Grand Canyon with a snorting laugh, and Cara humored my pathetic joke with a grin. "Was it always there? I feel like I've made the big changes that I meant to make in my life and neglected the little ones."

Cara was nodding. "I feel like maybe I've done the opposite, that I filled up my life with little things that improve my day without considering the massive things that made me unhappy."

"Yeah."

"Yeah. So what do we do now?"

"I have no idea."

After a time, Cara asked softly, "Do you still love her?"

I took a deep breath before I answered, trying to put words to something that up to now, I'd only felt. "I don't know. Maybe. It's like I should be able to stop all at once, but that's harder than it sounds. I kind of…I kind of don't want my life going forward to be about missing her or hating her. I don't even want this week to be about that. My life is bigger than her, and it always has been." I stopped, pressing my palms into the warm rock.

Cara listened intently, not rushing to fill the silences. I liked that about her, I realized, but her silence drew words out of me like no one I'd ever met. I'd barely even spoken to my parents about Bridget, past saying that she was an ugly cheater and her nose was unnaturally small, a fact that I had carried in silence for years, and that I never wanted to talk about her again. They respected that, but maybe they shouldn't have. Maybe I shouldn't have asked. Maybe I should've had a real conversation with the people who loved me most in the world.

"What about you?" I asked.

Cara shook her head. "Oh, I definitely don't love Bridget."

I pushed her to the side, and she laughed, straightening. But in the seconds that followed, her face grew serious, then sad.

"I just wanted to save our marriage," she said. "That was my whole goal. I couldn't stand the thought of telling our families that it was over. I would wake up at night in a complete panic, and he would pretend to still be sleeping." She cringed, then went on, "I used to wonder all the time, what if he was someone else, Enrique or someone I'd see at the gym, and I'd imagine this whole other life for myself, and since I was imagining, I could make it be…more, be better than what I had. After a while, I never wanted to come back to reality. I think…" She took a full breath in and out. "I think that I stopped loving Lorenzo a long time ago."

"You were really unhappy," I said, a little surprised. Had Bridget been that unhappy? It wouldn't excuse her being a lying, cheating bag of trash, but maybe I should've wondered, before now, if that was part of the reason she turned to Lorenzo. Maybe our marriage had already been failing.

"Yes. But I don't think I realized it, or I didn't let myself think those actual words. I would've done anything to save my marriage.

Anything. And that was the focus of all my thoughts and all my energy, until…until his bags were packed. He left the apartment key on the counter, and when he was gone, I sat there and held it. I had never felt so powerless."

"And now?"

"Now what?" Cara asked.

"Would you take him back if he asked?"

She was shaking her head before my sentence was finished. "I think they both showed us who they are. I don't think we can pretend, anymore, not to know."

We sat in silence for a long time, staring out at the unearthly beauty of the canyon. It should've felt wrong to have such a sad conversation in the midst of such a wonder, but instead, I stared at the layers of stone, the millennia underneath us, and it gave me a feeling of rightness I couldn't explain.

That was the hard part, not having the words. If I'd known what to say, I could've shared my thoughts with Cara, and it was strange to think that I *wanted* to share them with her badly.

After an hour, we weren't ready to abandon our private view of the canyon. Cara grabbed snacks, lamenting that she was already out of popcorn, and I brought out my guitar, listening for the echo of my chords below.

I'd been working on putting some of Mary Oliver's poems to music, not to break a whole lot of copyright laws, but just for me.

After a while, the sound of tires crunching gravel interrupted my strumming.

"Ladies! Ladies, excuse me. This is a restricted area."

Cara and I turned to find a small white man in a brown uniform emerging from the truck and bustling toward us. We looked at each other, then immediately looked around for a sign.

"I apologize," Cara sputtered. "We were following the GPS and didn't see—"

"Two pretty girls like you? You gotta use your brain and not those damned computers, don't ya? Never know where you'll end up." He spoke to her breasts and adjusted his belt. I'd seen power-mad police officers do the same thing, but this asshat didn't have a gun or a badge, just ill-fitting clothes and a sadistic tilt to his grin. "Never seen anyone on this road who wasn't a park ranger or a troublemaker. Or an axe murderer, but just the one. Now, you girls—"

I was done with this conversation. If I wanted to be ogled and talked down to by gross old white men, I'd go into politics. I turned toward the car, but I knew I wouldn't be taking a step away from Cara unless she was following. "Come on, we'll go ahead to the next public area."

"That's forty miles back the way you came," he said, pointing his thumb over his shoulder. "All the way back to the *posted* lookout points. 'Round here, there's no rails, no guards. Anything at all could happen to a couple of pretty things like you. I could tell you some stories. I've been a park ranger twenty-five years, and—"

I could tell him some stories, too, and many of them started with a friendly seeming stranger commenting on all the things that could happen to a couple of pretty things like us.

He took a step toward us. It seemed absent-minded, just shuffling his feet, but the alarm bells that had been tinkling started clanging.

"What about the other way?" Cara was asking, gesturing to the road ahead.

He frowned at her, then at her boobs. "Dead end. You gonna tell me you didn't see that sign either? Need glasses? Or maybe you need someone to show ya."

Cara seemed like she was about to apologize again, so I reached for her and turned her toward the car, gripping hard enough that she seemed to get my message. I had my guitar in one hand, but I didn't take my other hand off her shoulder until she was safely in the driver's seat.

He was still talking at us when we got in and started the engine.

I was trembling slightly as we drove away. It was strange. He'd been only vaguely threatening, but I lived in one of the largest cities in the country. I kept my own business open late. I didn't live in the nicest part of town. I was a woman. I was accustomed to dealing with vaguely threatening.

Maybe he'd just surprised me, showing up the way he did. Maybe his tone had been enough to signal to my brain that we might be in a dangerous situation. Maybe his gawking at Cara's chest made me want to run him over. It was hard to say.

Soon enough, I'd put him out of my mind, and half an hour later, we found the sign and the place where the lane split off from the main tourist road. I suppose I had just kept driving in the direction of the canyon, never noticing the two-foot wooden pole with the rusted *Restricted Area* sign the size of a dessert plate.

We stopped and took a selfie with it.

Chapter Nineteen

Cara and I made our way back to an approved viewing platform in time for sunset. The orange and red hues of the rock walls could've been fire—they were so vibrant. People crowded around us, holding up phones and cameras, speaking a variety of languages.

I couldn't help but pause my admiration of the view for a moment to appreciate how awesome it was that people all over the world were amazed by this natural wonder, too, a wonder that was relatively close to home, for me.

"I kind of wish that we'd planned to stay another day, maybe hike down at the bottom," Cara said, standing on tiptoe to peer over the railing next to a toddler trying to do the same.

"You said we're not on a bell schedule," I said. "We can, if you want."

A sudden cool wind hit us, and she took a step closer to me. The sun seemed to sink a little faster.

"I can't decide," she said.

I opened my mouth, then realized I was about to say that I didn't care what we did, as long as I was with her, then stopped. It was the sort of thing that I would've said to Bridget, months ago, trying to be accommodating. Maybe I hadn't yet gotten out of the habit.

I shook myself loose of the thoughts. "Let's go on tonight, then if we decide to hike on the way back, we'll have time to schedule a tour guide or whatever."

"Afraid you're going to get lost in the Grand Canyon?" she teased.

"I got lost driving *next to* the Grand Canyon. With our luck, we'd get in there, and no one but the javelinas and creepy old park rangers would find us."

Cara laughed and bumped me with her arm.

We stood still, barely touching, until the sun was completely gone.

❖

I woke in the morning to the feel of someone between my legs. I ran my hands over her soft skin, lightly then harder, wanting her pressed up against every inch of my skin. I'd imagined her kiss on my neck, but this was better, lips and tongue and teeth, my nerves strummed like guitar strings, leaving me vibrating.

My breathing was hard and fast, and my muscles tightened with anticipation. I felt my thighs clench, drawing that feeling, that someone, closer, tighter.

God, I'd been wanting…

Everything in me was spring-wound and ready to let go. I pressed my fingers into her soft curls. Palms—mine?—moved over my breasts, passing feather-like over my nipples.

For one indescribable moment, I felt her incredible lips against mine, and I arched, needing her, hungry for her. Touching her in all the ways she deserved to be touched, bringing her with me to the edge.

Finally.

In the next moment, I was fully awake, leaping out of bed in another strange hotel room, except there was a pillow between my legs, so I tripped and ended up on the floor, panting and bruised.

"Are you okay?" Cara peeked around the corner. She was already dressed and had a mouthful of foaming toothpaste. I stared at her foaming lips before trying to look away and getting my attention snagged by her headful of curls. The feeling of them between my fingers was so fresh and real that my hand flexed in response.

I said something, probably words, as I got to my feet.

I went straight past her, pushed her out the bathroom door, and took a shower.

❖

This would be the worst of our days on the road. There were no aliens or sand dunes or rabid javelinas to break up the day, just road and desert. I'd searched for some small tourist attraction, but the Stonehenge of broken cars—Carhenge, for those in the know—was in Nebraska, the world's largest beagle-shaped bed and breakfast was in Idaho, and Spoonbridge was all the way in Minnesota.

Cara and I vowed to keep an eye out for interestingly shaped cacti.

We drove through the morning in relatively good cheer, though my mind played the dream of making love to her on a loop, like a reel that I couldn't put down. And despite the awkwardness of fantasizing about her while she was sitting next to me, I didn't want to let it go.

Late in the morning, Cara talked me into duet karaoke. We were particularly good at "You're the One That I Want" from *Grease*, but our "Don't Go Breaking My Heart" was awful no matter which of us sang Kiki Dee's part and no matter how many times we practiced.

We stopped in a small town for a late lunch, then headed out into the empty desert again.

We drove another hour, then four. If there was anything out here but road, desert, and Cara's car, I couldn't see any evidence.

Eventually, Cara sighed dramatically. "Can we just stop? I've got to get out of the car for a minute."

Just as she spoke, a building appeared ahead, a convenience store with a single car in the parking lot.

I pointed to it. "What do you think about *not* peeing in the sand?"

"Yes, please."

I parked at the fuel pump to refill the tank, then we trekked over the sand-speckled parking lot. It was grungy inside, even for a convenience store, and most of the overhead lights were out, but they had an antique popcorn machine in pristine condition.

"Does it work?" Cara asked the cashier.

"You betcha. Want a bucket? You'll have to wait a minute or five for the oil to heat."

Cara glanced at me, her eyes wide with pleading.

"We're not in a hurry," I reminded her.

We browsed the store while the cashier bustled around the machine, opening the glass door and waiting until just the right moment to send the kernels clicking into the pot.

Cara held up a yellow resin keychain with a scorpion inside. "Souvenir?"

"No, thank you. The candy bar and the restroom hepatitis will be plenty for me today."

The cashier called, "Order up!" and handed us two red-and-white striped paper containers overflowing with popcorn. Cara and I dropped at least ten pieces each before we made it back outside.

"Whose turn is it to drive?" I asked.

Cara stopped in front of the car. "Is it bad that I'd rather sleep on the ground than get back into that thing right now?"

"How far away do you think they had to go to get one of those scorpions?"

"Good point."

"We can switch in another hour, if you don't want to drive yet."

"Thanks." She got back into the car, on the passenger side.

I drove, but not far. We'd passed several dirt turnoffs with tire tracks, places where drivers could pull well off the road without worrying about getting stuck in the sand. I stopped at the next one.

"What are you doing?" Cara asked through a mouthful of popcorn.

"Looking for scorpions. Want to help?"

"Not even a little." But she got out of the car, and when I climbed onto the roof, dangling my feet over the side, she climbed up, too, popcorn still in hand.

I could almost feel a breeze up there. Around us, I could see nothing but desert and the sinking sun and the distant mountains ahead of us, which maybe wasn't the greatest reminder of how far left we had to go. What had felt monotonous when I was behind the wheel was something completely different here, where I could lean back and feel the sun on my eyelids and the prickling of sand on my face when the wind picked up.

Cara leaned against me for a moment, her head on my shoulder. I tried not to savor the feeling, tried not to feel bereft as she sat straight and took a deep breath of the dry, hot air.

"Thank you," she said and shoved another handful of popcorn into her mouth.

We sat in the quiet, listening to the wind and the occasional hawk cry, watching the sky come alive with color as the sun set.

❖

At last, we reached our last day of driving before we'd settle into our cabin in the redwoods.

I didn't know about Cara, but I was so ready to be there, to be out of the car for a few days, to have slow morning coffee under the trees instead of whatever we could grab on the road. I wanted to use my legs on a more regular basis, and I didn't want to see or hear or smell that orange car again until we had to drive home.

I called my parents from the car while Cara filled the gas tank.

"Hello, Dad," I said cautiously. "You're not still telling your religious jokes, are you?"

"No. *Namaste* serious. Okay, that was the last one."

I laughed. "Thank goodness. How are you? How's Mom?"

"Didn't you talk to her like two days ago? What is this, caring-about-your-parents week?"

"I care about you all the time. I'm just not often so far away that I can't help if I need to."

Dad blew a raspberry into the phone. "We don't need you, kiddo."

"I know," I said, and I mostly meant it. Usually, they only needed me for tech support, and not often even for that. They were still young and fit, for parents, but that didn't mean that I was ignorant of the way they were aging.

"Hey, I learned a cool trick. I'll show you when you visit, but the gist is, whenever your mother starts getting on my nerves, I turn on a cricket game, and she goes away within five minutes. I found one of those TV apps that's twenty-four hour cricket, seven days a week cricket. It's magic."

"That's a pretty cool trick," I admitted. "Do you actually like cricket?"

"I like it a lot now that it gets me out of lectures about my blood pressure. How does she think yelling at me is going to help with my blood pressure, exactly?" He snorted a laugh.

"She's a mystery."

"She's a…a beautiful woman. Majestic. And wise."

"Hi, Mom," I said, loud enough that I knew she'd be able to hear.

"Here," Dad said. "Talk to your daughter. She's screeching like someone stepped on her tail."

There was a rustle of movement, then Mom's voice. "Why are you torturing your poor father? Don't you know that's my job?"

Dad said, "Hah!" from the background.

Badger yipped in solidarity. My heart squeezed pathetically at the sound.

"Yes, she misses you, too," Mom said, ostensibly to the dog. "Are you tired of driving yet?" she asked me.

"Very," I said, watching Cara lean against the car with her hand on the pump. "But it's been worth it."

We chatted for a minute about the Grand Canyon and Mom's garden. She had never seen the Grand Canyon, but she had read about it extensively since she heard I was going there and had almost as many facts to give me as Cara. She also couldn't wait until I was back home so she could give me a whole bagful of weird kinds of cucumbers from her garden, and I pretended to want them.

Maybe Cara liked cucumbers and could take them off my hands.

Mom held Badger up to the phone so I could hear his snuffling breaths. Then we said good-bye.

I wasn't used to feeling homesick. It took me a minute to identify the feeling.

Cara climbed back into the car, windswept and slightly sweaty. She grinned at me, and I very nearly reached over to smooth her hair. We'd become comfortable together, sharing the same space, but not that comfortable. Not that intimate.

She was lovely, though, with her curls a mess, like she'd just climbed out of bed after a very well-spent afternoon. Just like she'd been in my dream.

"What?" she asked.

"What?" I mimicked.

"You're staring at me."

"You're staring at me," I mimicked again, unable to come up with anything not stupid to say.

She had this lacy pocket on the front of her shirt, and I realized that she had a lot of clothes like that, with a hint of lace or embroidery here or there, sort of like an old lady, but in an utterly charming way.

I turned away quickly before she could accuse me of staring at her chest.

Some Puritan ancestor whispered in my head that she shouldn't be so pretty. It was a temptation to sin.

Then I spent a lot of time thinking about what that would be like, sinning with Cara Espinoza.

Thick gray clouds filled the sky as we headed out of town, making the day so dark that we had to depend on the headlights to see the road ahead. Fat raindrops spattered with an unreasonably loud sound, as though they had been hurled down from the sky instead of just falling.

"We'll probably drive right out of it," Cara said.

"I'm sure it's just a little rainstorm," I said, but I might not have been convincing.

"Does the weather stress you out?" Cara asked.

"A little. I don't know why. I probably watched *Twister* too many times. I also watched *Titanic* too many times. I spent years terrified of boats. And Kate Winslet."

"Do you want me to drive?" she asked.

"No, but thank you. Just distract me. Give me one of your road trip conversation topics."

"How about…" She scrolled through her phone. "Where's the weirdest place you've had sex?"

"Where are you getting these questions?" I asked, my voice squeaking. I wasn't sure I could handle talking about sex with her right now, not with us so close and yet not nearly close enough. The center console between us was a thin but impermeable force field.

"Do you think that's a weird question?" Cara asked thoughtfully. "I thought it was fun. I'll go first. Mine is probably the foreign languages section of my college library. Do you know what countries speak Tagalog? Or maybe it was that time at the Natural History Museum. I don't know what qualifies as weird, exactly. But we were behind a mammoth fossil, so that seems pretty weird." She paused. "It had really, really big tusks."

After a moment, she turned in my direction and saw me gaping at her, before I refocused on the road.

"What?" she asked.

"Cara Espinoza. I never would have imagined you were a *bad* girl."

"Shut up," Cara said.

"No, I'm serious. I am so surprised that if you literally told me right now that you were three raccoons disguised as a human, that would be less surprising than what I just heard come out of your mouth."

Cara smiled, then wrinkled her nose. I needed to stop looking at her and watch the road, but it had never been more difficult. "I do seem to give off a goody-goody vibe, don't I?" she asked. "I just figured you were able to see through that." She almost sounded disappointed in me, which amused me even more for some reason.

"I'm starting to," I said. "You do have that sweet innocent teacher thing going on for you. But I guess you can't judge a slut by her cover."

She slapped my arm, laughing. "No way. You are not going to shame me for having a good time in my twenties. Especially not when I know you were having just as much fun."

"Oh yes, *I* definitely give off the opposite of a good girl vibe," I admitted. "But I've never knocked boots anywhere more adventurous than the beach."

"Seriously? I always imagined…Never mind." She looked down and started fiddling with her phone.

"No," I told her. "You can't stop there. You imagined what? That I was doing it next to the dinosaur fossils, too?"

"Honey," she said gently, "mammoths aren't dinosaurs. You know that, right?"

"Yeah, whatever."

"So what beach was it where you got…adventurous?" Cara asked.

"Bolivar Flats. Have you been out there? It's usually deserted except for the bird-watchers. It's just miles of sand and waves. It's beautiful."

"So that's who you hooked up with on the beach? Some bird-watcher?"

I shook my head vehemently. "Never. I have zero tolerance for standing there while someone talks about migration and beak shapes. I would literally rather be shot in a nonvital organ. I would rather subsist on your granola bar bricks. I would rather—"

"Yeah, I got it. So, not a bird-watcher. Then who?"

I wrinkled my nose. "Bridget. It was a few years ago, when we were going through a rough time, just arguing constantly. So I thought I should do something romantic, something new. I *had* planned a picnic."

"So, what happened?" Cara asked, catching my word choice. Not

We had a picnic. Nope. It was, again, a good idea that hadn't panned out. Our marriage, in a nutshell.

I squinted into the rain. "I packed a basket of her favorite foods. We got frisky on the beach. She said it was sandy. We walked a little farther. She complained about the wind, the temperature of the water on her bare feet, and the lack of pretty seashells. Then she stepped on a jellyfish. According to her, everything was ruined. The whole thing was a disaster. She would tell the story later like I'd deliberately planned the worst date of our lives."

"I'm sorry," Cara said gently.

"She said that she would never go anywhere again that wasn't the seawall in Galveston."

"Where it's crowded all the time and smells like petroleum?"

"Yep," I said, though I usually loved Galveston. It was a fascinating and fun place with a kick-ass homemade candy store, but not a good destination for getting lucky on a sand dune. "And where you can get a cocktail quickly when you get attacked out of nowhere by a malicious jellyfish."

Cara was silent for a minute, which stretched into two. I suddenly realized why.

"You want to give me an interesting fact about jellyfish, don't you?" I asked, resigned.

"The smallest jellyfish species can't be seen without a magnifying glass, and the largest can be more than six feet across and one hundred feet long," she said quickly, as though afraid I might change my mind. Then she whispered, "And box jellyfish have twenty-four eyes."

I laughed. "That is very interesting, Cara. Thank you."

Soon, we stopped seeing small towns and traffic lights and, eventually, any other signs of civilization. We drove for hours in the drizzling rain through a flat desert with scrubby, dead-looking bushes. There were mountains in the distance and the occasional abandoned motel, but nowhere to even consider pulling over except the bare roadside when the storm worsened.

The rain grew so loud on the roof of the car that we could hardly hear the thunder. I watched the lightning, looking in those brief flashes for funnel clouds, though I had no idea if they had tornadoes in Arizona or California or wherever we were.

We'd been on the road at least an hour without seeing another car or building when there was a pop of electricity, and everything in the car turned off. The display screen was dark. There were no lights on the dash. The fan was silent.

Cara and I looked at each other.

She pushed the gas. Nothing happened.

Slowly, the car coasted. Cara steered it onto the shoulder, over the rumble strips, and stopped, shifting into park.

We sat for a moment in the quiet, listening to our own too-fast breaths and the snare drum roll of the rain.

"This is unfortunate," I said.

Cara glared at me, opening her mouth, no doubt to tell me I was useless, then changed her mind and settled on reaching for her phone. After a minute of tapping, she said, "No signal."

I stupidly checked my phone, with the same result.

Cara tried to start the car again, but nothing happened, not the slightest sound or flicker.

There was so little light that we could've been stuck in the damned elevator again if it wasn't for the overwhelming noise of the rain. Neither of us seemed eager to try to talk over the sound, but at last, I leaned closer to her ear, trying to tell myself that I wasn't going to take the opportunity to smell her hair.

"Stay with the car. I'll walk and see if I can pick up some cell reception in a mile or two."

"No," Cara said, shaking her head vehemently.

"What?"

"No, I'm not sitting here alone while you go off like we're characters in a horror movie. I'm coming with you."

"Fine," I huffed. "Come on, then."

With all the packing we'd done, it turned out that neither of us had thought to bring an umbrella. Cara had a jacket that at least looked waterproof. I settled for holding a plastic bag over my head.

We got out quickly, locked the doors, and hurried in the direction of California.

Within minutes, we were both shivering.

"How is it this cold?" Cara asked.

"Maybe we're at a higher elevation. Maybe a cold front brought the rain. Maybe—"

"Shut up. I know how weather works. I was just complaining."

"Oh," I said. The wind whipped the plastic bag out of my hands and instantly skyward. I wrapped my arms more tightly around myself. "In that case, how is it this fucking cold?"

"Do you think one of us is magnetic?" she asked.

"What?"

"First the elevator. Now the car."

"I doubt it," I said reasonably. "But I think I'll avoid air travel for a while."

I have no idea how long we walked. We stopped now and then to check for a signal. We'd put both of our phones into a mostly clean Tupperware container to keep them dry.

Finally, the rain stopped pounding and only drizzled. I was able to look around a little, especially as the clouds overhead thinned enough to allow some daylight. I was surprised that the sun was still overhead and not half hidden behind the mountains. I was sure we'd been out here for hours.

A movement beside the road startled Cara, and she took several fast steps back. I froze.

Several gigantic rabbits, bigger than your average cat, with angry faces had crawled out from under the roadside bushes and were eying us. They looked either wet or mangy, their fur matted like they'd just been washed out and hung up to dry.

"Jackrabbits," Cara said, as though she knew I'd ask.

"Vegetarian jackrabbits?" I whispered hopefully.

I had no idea how these monsters could be related to the cuddly bunnies at the pet store. They were closer to rabid kangaroos. One of them took a hop toward us with its freakishly huge feet. It looked hungry, too thin, and not nearly as frightened as we were.

In unison, the others hopped forward, too. I grabbed Cara's arm and took several steps backward, dragging her with me, not daring to turn my eyes away from their hungry black pupils.

The jackrabbits must have heard the car approaching before we did. In an instant, thirty of them were fleeing, their unnaturally long back feet flexing as they bolted away from us. Only after they vanished did Cara turn and start waving.

The massive RV honked once, and its brake lights were the most beautiful red. I felt breathless with relief. I knew that jackrabbits were probably far from the most dangerous creatures out here.

Then again, we were two women alone on a highway with a stranger stopping to pick us up. No doubt, we'd be safer with the jackrabbits, the javelinas, the bears, or whatever else was waiting for us in the darkness.

Still, I couldn't see a better option, and Cara had already started running to meet the RV.

It took the RV some distance to stop, but as soon as it was parked, both of the front doors swung wide open, and two elderly white people emerged and walked toward us, meeting at the back of the RV.

I sized them up and figured Cara and I could take them, if it came to that.

But they were both smiling, and Cara had already reached them.

"Caught in a rainstorm in the desert? Which gods did you piss off?" the woman said, her voice projecting over the empty road.

A moment later, I'd caught up with Cara and stood close to her, just in case.

"Mildred!" the man scolded, then turned to us. "I apologize for my sister, now and for the duration of our acquaintance."

"Need a ride, cursed ones?" she asked.

He put his head in his hands and turned away.

I was laughing in relief as I followed them to the door. They might still turn out to be axe murderers, but at least they would keep us entertained.

Mildred and Jeffrey were in their seventies, retired, and exploring North America. They gave us most of their life story before Cara and I could even tell them what we needed, but they were delightful, and it was clear that Mildred only acted the way she did because it embarrassed her little brother.

At Mildred's insistence, Cara and I took the two seats behind them, even though we were sure to leave puddles, and we buckled in.

To my surprise, Jeffrey offered to go back and get Cara's car.

"It's no trouble," Mildred said, turning the wheel and getting back on the road. "This thing is built to tow. Honestly, we should've been towing my car this whole way. It's a nightmare to get this whole thing in and out of the Starbucks parking lot."

"Where are you headed?" Jeffrey asked.

"Muir Woods," Cara said.

Jeffrey whistled. “That’s still quite a distance. Well, where’s home?”

“Houston,” I said, miserably.

“That’s even worse,” Mildred agreed. “Er, farther, I meant. We like Houston and love Muir Woods. But for now, we’ll get you to the nearest town with a service station, how’s that?”

“That is more than generous,” Cara said. “We can pay you.”

Mildred and Jeffrey laughed so hard that I thought we would crash.

“Mildred invested in Netflix’s IPO,” Jeffrey explained.

“In 2002,” Mildred said with a chortle, “back when they still sent you DVDs in the mail. Took a second mortgage out on the house, sold as much plasma as they’d take, and put all the cash into stocks.”

“Most foolish thing you ever did,” Jeffrey said. “What if it’d failed? Most businesses do, you know. And IPOs are risky as hell.”

Mildred glanced over her shoulder and winked at us. “Twenty-plus years, and he’s still going on about it. True, it took a dip that first year. Scared the bejeezus out of me. But since then…” Mildred whistled and drove her index finger straight up. “Through the roof!” she exclaimed.

Cara did exactly what I did, looking at Mildred and Jeffrey, then turning to look behind us at the interior of the fanciest RV we’d ever seen. There were leather recliners, a wall-sized TV, a full kitchen, and…was that a tiny chandelier? It was absurd. It was also larger than my first apartment.

“The shower has a skylight,” Mildred bragged.

Cara turned back to me, her hair and clothes dripping and plastered flat, makeup obliterated by the heavy rain, and laughed out loud. She must have been thinking of the absurdity of our situation, stranded on the side of the road, rescued by millionaires.

I took my phone out of the Tupperware. “Would you two like to be on our Mesmio?”

Chapter Twenty

After Cara explained Mesmio to Mildred and Jeffrey, much more patiently than I would've managed, they were excited to be a part of our road trip video blog, as Cara generously described it. I tended to think of it as proof of life for family members and random crap for our few dozen other followers.

I recorded Cara from my seat as she talked, then recorded Mildred's reaction, some travel tips from Jeffrey, and ended with a few anecdotes from Mildred.

"I almost got eaten by a moose!" she exclaimed. "But that's nothing. Jeffrey saw a Bigfoot."

"It was not Bigfoot," Jeffrey protested.

"You thought it was."

"Momentarily."

"What was it?" Cara asked, fascination in her voice. I glanced at her. No to aliens but yes to Bigfoot? What kind of sense did that make?

Mildred chortled. "A woman with curly hair in a fur coat. Jeffrey was hiding behind a bush taking her picture, and she was trying to relieve herself in privacy."

Cara and I were both laughing, and poor Jeffrey had the kind of translucent skin that couldn't conceal a blush.

Mildred started in on a new story before we'd gotten control of our laughter.

I was starting to worry that they would never stop talking when we, Cara's car included, slowed to a stop outside a shady-looking repair shop in a town whose name I didn't catch.

I offered to talk to the mechanic because Mildred wanted help putting the videotape app on her phone.

Cara agreed quickly enough that I suspected she, too, thought she was getting the better end of the deal.

❖

When I got back to the RV, Cara looked somber, though I was the one with the bad news.

"They said they won't even be able to take a look at it until tomorrow," I said. "But there's a motel and a diner across the street, so we won't have to sleep on the street *or* starve."

"I don't want to abandon you here," Mildred said.

"Mildred, we can't—"

"Shut your face, Jeffrey. I can do whatever I want."

"We'll be fine," Cara said hurriedly. "Really. You've helped us far more than we could've hoped, and I'm sure the car will be a quick fix." She glanced at me, then away, as though she didn't want to know if I disagreed.

Between my wet clothes and the RV's very effective air conditioning, I was visibly shivering by that point and unable to stop. Still, I tried to reassure Mildred and drag Cara away across the gravel parking lot at the same time.

The rain had stopped, at last, and the air felt marginally warmer.

"I'll send you a videotape on the phone as soon as I figure out how to make one," Mildred promised through her open window.

"She'll have it figured out in no time," Jeffrey said. "She's already a whiz at the *Candy Crush*."

Cara and I waved good-bye and went to unload our suitcases from her broken car.

"I'm sorry," I said, patting the hood.

"Are you talking to the car or to me?" Cara asked, grinning.

"Uh, you," I said quickly. "Normal people like me don't talk to cars, especially weird orange ones." I leaned down and said in a mock whisper, "I don't mean it. You're beautiful."

Cara rolled her eyes and led the way to the motel.

"What?" I said. "I'm allowed to change my mind. Bessie's a good car."

"Don't name her. And *Bessie*? Really?"

We were both ravenous, but too cold to consider sitting in a chilly diner until we both had a shower and put on dry clothes.

We got checked into the motel, which—surprise!—had an abundance of vacant rooms. By the time we lugged our suitcases inside, I was hungry enough to snack on one of Cara's peanut butter granola bar bricks.

We both groaned with relief when we got our wet shoes off, and we laughed at the synchronicity.

Cara said it was my turn to shower first, and I selfishly didn't argue.

I was pretty sure the tile in the bathroom was older than me, and the carpet around the beds was worn flat and slightly sticky. After my shower, I dressed in jeans and the only long-sleeved shirt I'd brought, then immediately put my shoes back on. I couldn't tell if the carpet had a pattern somewhere under the grime or just stains.

The room had a painfully loud window unit with a protruding fringe of mold, a beat-up mini fridge, a microwave that looked like it hadn't been safety tested since the 1960s, and no TV. Also no coffeepot, not even the crappy little single serving ones that weighed less than a banana.

And like a rom-com gone awry, there was one queen bed. And the bathroom didn't lock.

I recorded some sarcastic comments while Cara showered, leaving out the name of the poor motel that probably didn't see many visitors here in the middle of nowhere. But their disturbing holographic wall art demanded criticism.

I dried my hair with Cara's dryer, something I rarely bothered to do with my long, thick mess, but after spending the last several hours with wet hair, I was more than tired of the feeling. I closed my eyes as the heat took away the last of the chill from the rain.

When Cara still hadn't emerged, I dug out one of my Mary Oliver collections and read, but I was still too hungry to focus.

I patiently waited an entire thirty seconds after Cara was out of the bathroom before asking, "Ready for food?"

"I need like five minutes for makeup," she said, digging in her suitcase. She was wearing jeans with embroidered flowers at the hem and a tight yellow shirt that brought out the gold in her eyes.

"You're beautiful just as you are."

"You're starving, I know. Just mascara. I promise."

"*Soooo* beautiful."

She rolled her eyes, and I watched her brush her wet hair and darken her eyelashes, which seemed to make absolutely no difference. I made a little dancing movement toward her with the red lipstick I'd bought in New Mexico, and she rolled her eyes at me again. But she put it on.

"Oh my God, can I have your autograph?" I breathed.

She laughed, a shockingly lovely sight with her bright red lips. "You're so weird."

We ordered far too much food at the diner. Cara, too, must have noticed the dented mini fridge in the motel room. Our young waiter—*Lane (they/them)*, according to the words in thick black marker under the diner logo—wore a blue and white checkered diner dress, complete with a lace-edged apron. They were probably in their early twenties, with sparkly blue eyeshadow and neatly combed goatee. They looked from Cara to me and then at the long list on their order pad and just shook their head.

"I think Lane doubts our hunger," I said.

"I think they doubt our stomach capacity, and they may have a point. What do you think, Lane? Did we overdo it?"

Lane looked at us both again, the goatee not quite disguising their smile. "I have faith in you," they said, then took our order to the kitchen.

When I turned back to Cara, she was looking at me.

"What?"

"Do you always learn everyone's name?"

I shrugged. "It's a good business practice, when you can learn your regulars. Makes them feel special."

"Hmm," she said, still looking at me.

I took my phone out of my pocket and snapped her picture.

"Stop. I look like a wet rat."

I snapped one of her with an angry face and turned my phone around so she could see.

"This is perfect," I said. "It's quintessential Cara, mad at me for being so charming. That's what the description will say."

"I do rock the lipstick," she said, examining the photo.

"You do. Now tell me what Mildred did to freak you out."

"What?"

"After I talked to the mechanic—Bill, by the way—I came back to the RV, and you looked like you'd seen a ghost. Not just a ghost, the ghost of a tax auditor asking to see your last five years' returns."

"Hah, accountant joke," she said, then grew serious. "It wasn't Mildred." Cara looked at her phone, and at first I thought she was ignoring me, but then she turned it so I could see.

It was our Mesmio profile. In our profile picture, we are in bright sunlight. I'm laughing with my mouth wide open, and Cara is rolling her eyes at me. There is a glimpse of shining white behind us, and I realized we were at White Sands National Park.

Right then, I thought: That's the picture I'll get printed from this trip. We look happy and carefree, and God, I'd love to have a picture beside my bed that doesn't have Bridget in it.

I shook my head. "What am I…?"

But then I saw it. We had passed one hundred thousand followers and half a million likes.

"Whoa," I said, feeling the same nausea that Cara must have felt when she first saw those numbers. I read them again, counting the individual digits to be sure. But there it was. Not a thousand, not ten thousand, one hundred thousand.

"It's a good thing," Cara said, her voice a little high.

"Sure," I said. "But…why, exactly?"

Cara met my eyes across the table. "I don't know."

I thought about it until Lane brought our food, and then I focused on my French toast and hash browns because I have my priorities straight in life.

"It doesn't change anything," I said, once we had finished our first platefuls. "The numbers, I mean," I said.

"Right." Cara stabbed a sausage. "We just keep recording for the sake of the trip. Then we're done."

For the sake of the trip. For our *show the world we're fine* plan. For our exes.

It was funny how quickly they'd ceased to be the point.

Honestly, the only reason I could come up with for continuing to record at all was that I wanted these memories of our trip. I wanted to thumb through them when we got home, and again in a year, and in five years. I wanted to remember the amazing time when I got to see a little more of the world and got to know Cara better. I didn't want to forget a single moment.

Except for the terrifying jackrabbits. I would happily forget them.

Too soon, we'd be home. It was probably too late to see Muir Woods. We'd be back in Houston in a few days, back to real life.

I pictured the envelope on my desk and the alternate reality of this week, the one where Cara never walked through the door of Strings & Things. The one where I spent a week trying not to fall apart, desperate to keep my business and my home, sleeplessly holding all the what-ifs in my hands.

What if I'd loved Bridget better?

What if she'd loved me, too?

In this reality, those weren't the important questions. These were: What if I'd never gotten to spend this time with Cara? What if I'd never heard her laugh or sing or snore? I couldn't stand the thought. I wasn't perhaps on the vacation of my dreams, stuck here in a town from a Stephen King novel, but I was undeniably better off than I would've been at home, actually dealing with my problems like a boring, responsible adult.

After we were both full of greasy food, we took our doggie bags and walked slowly back to the motel. The night was cool, nice in comparison to the heavily air-conditioned diner. I wondered if Cara still felt the chill of being out in the rain and if there were extra blankets hidden somewhere in the motel room.

It was fully dark now and more evident than ever that we were in the smallest of small towns. There were four streetlights, the motel light, and the restaurant light, which switched off a few minutes after we left. The auto repair shop was dark, and the few houses we could see had nothing more than a lamp or two shining through the windows.

I looked up and stopped completely, gasping out loud. I reached out for Cara's arm to stop her, too. She looked at me, then followed my gaze.

I could see maybe ten stars from my house in the Houston suburbs.

Here, there were billions. They shone in faint colors, not uniform in size or shade as I'd always assumed before. Here, I could see that they were rich in variety, merging in a bright path across the middle of the sky.

"There's no moon tonight," Cara whispered. She hadn't pulled away from my hand, and I was glad because nothing else rooted me under that vast wonder. She was so close that I could smell her shampoo, not whatever miniature bottles the motel offered, but her own, a fruity smell with a hint of coconut. I took a deep breath, moving an inch closer.

I would swear that I could feel the heat of her body from where I stood. We were only ever a couple of feet apart in her tiny car, but it was nothing like this, standing so close to her, aware of exactly where her body would touch mine if she would take one more step.

"I don't want to be weird," I whispered back, still looking straight up at those incredible stars, "but I'd like to kiss you right now."

Instantly, my heart started pounding like I'd just finished running from a javelina. Had I actually just said that? The impulse to do something or say something, to touch her and kiss her and pull her against me, had been strong and growing. I just hadn't realized that the impulse was about to jump out of my mouth and possibly make the rest of this trip extraordinarily awkward.

Cara looked at me, but she didn't seem startled. She didn't move away. Her eyes moved from my eyes to my mouth and back again, and I felt her gaze like a touch. I shivered.

"Our room has one bed," she said.

"Yes," I said, my thumping heart suddenly very much liking where this conversation was going.

"Like a bad rom-com setup."

"Yes?" I asked, like maybe that was a good thing?

"Then, no. At least," Cara said, sounding thoughtful, "at least, not today. Ask me again tomorrow?"

Then she kept walking toward the motel as though that was a normal request.

"Okay," I said and followed her, my attention still torn between the sky and Cara.

Chapter Twenty-one

Was I dense? That was the question I went to sleep and woke up with, Cara breathing deeply beside me under every blanket we could find.

I mean, I was undeniably dense. Cara and I had been through the demolition of two marriages this year. We were stuck in a crappy motel several states away from home. And while I liked Cara…oh, I liked Cara. I liked her outrageously. I liked her like food and breathing.

The feeling came over me like going underwater. I thought I was just dipping my toe, but no, I was submerged.

I cared about her in a way that came with a whopping dose of attraction, so obvious that I didn't know how I'd managed to hide it from her. Maybe I hadn't.

I vividly remembered every time she'd touched me, in the cave dwellings, in the elevator, at the Grand Canyon, even taking the keys from her hand at the garage, as though without my knowing, my own memory had highlighted those moments for later study.

I watched her long, dark eyelashes, the way her hair had stuck to her face in dark curls and had gotten flattened against the pillow, the way her incredible lips parted in sleep. My whole body ached to move closer to hers.

"Can I kiss you *now*?" I whispered.

Her eyes didn't open, but the corner of her mouth twitched. "I haven't brushed my teeth. Believe me, you do not want to."

We opted for diner leftovers for breakfast, then had an hour to kill before the auto repair shop opened.

It was nice, in a way, not to spend the whole morning driving. I stretched every muscle in my body, peed as often as I wanted to, and lounged around with my guitar.

I played a parody of "Pocketful of Sunshine," slowing it down and playing it mournfully. Cara loved it and recorded a clip for our Mesmio. I promised to screw up some of her other favorite songs, for the sake of social media.

And I watched her move around the room, fix her hair, play on her phone, stretch out on the bed. I watched her walk and bend and turn. I watched her arms and her ass and her breasts and the lovely curve of her cheek.

"Stop," she said.

"Totally not my fault," I said, grinning and trying to tear my eyes away from her body.

My phone rang before we left the hotel. "Just a second," I told Cara, returning to the room. "It's my parents."

"Honey! Your dadi ma learned how to use Mesmio so she could watch your videos," Dad said as soon as I answered the phone.

"Really?" I asked. "Grandma Singh is so awesome." She was also approaching one hundred years old. She shared a birthday with Eartha Kitt.

"Yes!" Dad said. He was full of exclamations. "She says that you are beautiful and that she is so glad that you're enjoying your trip, but that she likes watching cooking Mesmio reels more."

I laughed and turned to Cara, wishing that I'd put the call on speakerphone. She waited in the doorway, looking at me with a slight smile in her eyes. And…a slight heat? It might have been wishful thinking. "That's wonderful," I said to Dad. "Tell her I'll try to learn how to cook so my videos are more interesting."

Cara laughed, too, nodding in agreement.

"I will," Dad said. "I told her that she should be the one making videos. Those white yoga girls would love to learn real Indian cooking."

"Dad!"

"What? I married one. Do you think your mother would be offended by being called a white yoga girl?"

"No, but she's gotten used to you. For everyone else, let's err on the safe side of not calling people that. How about *Indian cuisine enthusiasts*?"

He blew a raspberry. "You sound like your mother. You look like her, too. Where are my genes, hmm?"

"I look like you, too, Dad. We have exactly the same hair."

"And you went and dyed it purple so you could be cooler than me. Thanks a lot."

"I have extra dye if you're interested."

He snorted a laugh. "Let's do it. Don't tell your mother. I want it to be a surprise."

"It's a deal. How's Badger?"

"I don't know. He likes your mother more than me. I even fed him bacon under the table this morning, and he still likes her more."

"Don't feed him bacon. It's not good for him."

"It's not good for me either, but YOLO, you know?"

Cara was still waiting patiently, listening to me talk, but I was eager, too, to find out what the mechanic had to say about her car. I wouldn't mention anything to my parents until I had more news. *Hey, I broke down several states away* isn't what parents want to hear from their children.

Dad was still on the line, trying to turn YOLO into a yodel.

"And on that note, I'll talk to you later," I said.

"Wait," he said, "say hi to Dadi Ma on your next video. She'll get a kick out of that."

"I absolutely will. Thanks, Dad."

I hung up, and Cara and I walked to the repair shop. I thought about calling the music store again while we walked, but I didn't want to check in too often. Besides, Florence had said everything was *finer than frog hair split four ways*, which I assumed was a good thing.

Doug had been restringing guitars, his favorite task. He'd been at the store every time I called. I knew I could cover payroll this month and next, but past that…I tried to put it out of my mind. I'd decided to talk to them when I got home. There was no point dwelling on it until then.

When we got to the auto repair shop, Mechanic Bill recognized me and met us just inside. He wore grimy yellow coveralls, the same as yesterday, as far as I could tell.

"It's the battery," he said without preamble, "and we don't have a replacement in stock."

"Oh no." Cara closed her eyes. "How long?"

He looked us both in the eye and didn't sugarcoat it. "A week, minimum. Supply chain issues."

Cara shook her head and kept shaking it.

"Ah," I said to Bill, moving a little in front of Cara to give her a moment to process, "How do you feel about being on Mesmio?"

Our Mesmio reels with Mildred and Jeffrey had been fun, but I confess, it was the enormous number of views and followers that prompted me to ask. The burden of fame.

It turned out that our new friend Bill had an automotive repair Mesmio of his own.

"Do you want to stay or go back to the motel?" I asked Cara. "You can have some time on your own if you need."

She shook her head. "No, it's fine. Let's start recording."

Cara and I explained our spring break road trip to Bill and his followers. For ours, Bill told a funny anecdote about a car that wouldn't start and turned out to have a whole litter of baby possums curled up on top of the engine block. He was considerably more loquacious on camera.

"They were cute as a fluffle of bunnies," Bill said.

I didn't try to hide my grin.

I wondered if anyone besides me could tell that Cara's smile was fake.

I imagined that anyone who vividly remembered having vacation plans ruined by unexpected car repairs would probably realize. And sympathize. I didn't know what to feel yet.

I'd told my parents about our Mesmio page, but I doubted they'd seen our reels. If they were watching, my plan not to tell them about our car trouble had been a little pointless.

Once Cara had agreed to the repair and our videos were finished, I walked with her back across the street for coffee and pie. The diner was a much nicer place to hang out than the motel, and there didn't seem to be any other businesses besides a chain convenience store and a church.

We took the same wine-red booth as yesterday, both of us looking out the window and, likely, both wondering what on earth we were going to do now.

"Our trip," Cara said slowly, "is over."

"I know." I grimaced. "I'm sorry."

She dropped her head to the table, then immediately raised it, rubbing at her forehead. The table did look a little sticky. "It's not like there's an airport nearby, Honey," she said combatively, as though I'd disagreed with her. "Or even a car rental place."

I just kept nodding. "We'd probably spend the price of a plane ticket getting a rideshare or a taxi to the nearest airport, if it was even possible."

"I don't see what choice we have, really. We're stuck." She looked so morose, I wanted to cry. "I had just started to feel…like this was working, you know? I've spent the last decade following Lorenzo's plans, not really making any of my own. Do you know what that's like?"

I didn't know if she was really asking me, so I waited until she looked up questioningly.

"Yes," I said, then, "no. I always felt like I made all the plans with Bridget, and if I didn't, then nothing would ever happen. We'd just be sitting there on the couch until we died. I was the one who couldn't live that way, who demanded that we spend the weekend at a lake cabin or…or, God, start a music shop. Bridget was good at work, and she was a huge help getting the store started. But it was like, once she got home, she didn't have the effort for it. For us."

Cara was smiling slightly. "Yeah, I can see that in you. You'd always be like, *Let's sled down this sand dune* and *Let's poke this javelina and see if it chases us*." Her voice was deep and nasal when she mimicked me, completely unlike my very normal voice, which was lovely and melodic.

"I did not," I said, laughing.

"But you didn't bully Bridget into any of those things, did you? Never mind, I know the answer to that. You'd push if she wanted to be persuaded or swept away, if she'd wanted to feel wanted, but if you had a plan to go somewhere, and she didn't want to go, you'd have…"

"Gone anyway," I said. "Usually. Hypothetically. I haven't thought much about actual travel these last few years. Everything has been about the store." Still, I'd gone back to Bolivar Flats to walk those solitary beaches, alone. I'd gone to restaurants Bridget hadn't wanted to try. I'd even taken a couples' sushi-making class by myself because I wanted to learn how to make sushi, damn it. I'd invited Florence along that time, but it never would've occurred to me to *not* go.

"You'd have gone anyway," Cara agreed. "Gone alone. I've never done that, Honey. I think this is the first time in my life I've ever picked up a map and made a choice. And now it's over. I am not ready for it to be over."

"I am sorry," I repeated. "I guess hanging out for a week in this little hamlet isn't your idea of an adventure."

She let out all her breath. "I mean, it's not my living room. That's better than nothing. What are you going to do, being stuck here?"

"The music store's in good hands. It's your job I'm worried about."

Cara stared into the distance. "I have some time off. I only took a day or two this year."

I didn't comment on how resilient she must be to deal with the end of her marriage and still keep working. Resilient or stubborn. No, resilient *and* stubborn.

"One thing," I said. "I adore our one-bed situation, for the record. But I desperately do not want to stay in that filthy motel another night."

Cara sat up straighter, accepting my declaration as a challenge, and raised her hand to wave to Lane, who had their coffee decanter in one hand and two mugs in the other, like they'd foretold our arrival. "Lane, you wouldn't happen to know of another hotel nearby?"

Lane shook their head, approaching our table. "That's the only one. It's…a bit of an antique."

Cara's posture lost some of its strength. "That's a polite way of putting it. We seem to be stuck here for a while, and we're not exactly enjoying our stay. Present company excluded, of course," she hurried to add.

Lane's smile twitched, and they started pouring our coffee. "Not a hotel for fifty miles at least. But my mom owns a vacation rental about twenty miles out."

Cara looked at me, eyebrows raised.

"Um," I said, imagining a shed with a cot and little else, "could we take a look?"

Chapter Twenty-two

"Dear goodness," Cara said.

I was thinking the same, but with less restraint.

Lane's mom, it turned out, was the only veterinarian in the county, and she rented out her new, professionally decorated, spacious four-bedroom house while she was at conferences and on the very long vacations she took several times a year.

"You're in luck," Lane said. "It's usually booked months in advance, but the guests that were supposed to come this week canceled. Something about deciding that they couldn't stand to be in the same house for another second? That they would rather eat deep-fried batteries than share one more meal? That they would rather sleep with a bale of barbed wire than with each other? Something like that. Anyhoo. Too late for a refund. I'll ask to be sure, but since you're in a jam, I'm sure Mom will let you stay for free."

Cara gave a hiccuping gasp. I took a step closer to her, worried that the marble countertops were about to bring her to tears.

"It's gorgeous," I said, "but this is the middle of nowhere. Why is it usually booked?"

Lane gave me a confused look. "Because of the hot springs, of course."

Now *I* was about to cry.

"You're an angel, Lane," I said, taking the key and the takeout containers of pie from their hands. "A hero. A saint. You saved our vacation."

"Please let your mom know how grateful we are," Cara said. "We can pay her. And we'll make sure it's sparkling clean before we leave."

"Don't worry about that," Lane said, grinning. "My cousin does the housekeeping, and he's an absolute tool. Feel free to invite friends, throw a party, spill some wine. He'll never get it out of the carpet. Ready to go back to town and get your bags?"

We were. Lane had driven us over in what they called their classic VW Bug, not seeming to understand the difference between *classic* and *decrepit*. There were so many dents and spots of peeled paint that I could honestly tell what the last four colors had been. But I didn't complain, and neither did Cara, even though the road back to town was dirt and gravel and the VW had WWII-era shocks.

At the motel, we tossed clothes and shampoos and makeup into suitcases and bags, not caring whose was what, so long as none of it touched the contaminated carpet.

There may have been some spontaneous squeals of happiness, but I'd never swear to it.

I kept looking over at Cara, so overwhelmingly pleased to see her happy that I momentarily forgot that I was happy for other reasons, too—for a beautiful guesthouse, for hot springs, and more than anything else in my life, to not have to spend another second in this motel.

We waddled to the lobby with our load of bags. Cara passed the keys across the desk to the manager with carefully concealed glee.

"I hope you enjoyed your stay," the manager said.

"Mmph," she managed through closed lips.

I was openly laughing.

Lane helped us wedge our luggage into one side of the back seat and, when it was clear that wasn't going to be enough, stacked on top of my feet and lap. I could rest my chin on my guitar case.

"You look squished, Honey. Do you want to switch me? I can—" Cara started.

"There is a hot spring," I whispered. "Get in the car fast, and we might have time to see it before dark."

Cara got in fast.

Lane gave us walking directions to the hot spring as they drove to the house. They said, "You can't miss it," so many times that I started to get nervous.

They'd already given us the tour of the house, so as soon as we arrived and they'd helped us unload everything into the living room, they left to get back to the diner.

"I know you guys are stuck here without a car. If you want food, just call the diner and I'll drop it by. I live right over there." They gestured vaguely, getting back into their rickety car.

We effused thanks.

"If I ever have a child," Cara said, as we waved from the front door, "I'm naming them Lane."

"At first, I thought you said you were going to have one with Lane," I said, "which would not happen. They're way out of your league."

"Gee, thanks. I'd be more likely to adopt Lane. They're probably young enough to be my kid."

"No way. You're what, twenty-one?"

Cara shoved me gently. "I'm thirty-six, and I hate that you can say that and it feels like a compliment."

"I know it. Society is screwed up. Thirties are way better than twenties."

"In every possible way. Can you imagine us at forty? Fifty? We'll be unstoppable."

We stopped talking right inside the front door, staring down at our pile of luggage.

"Deal with it later?" I suggested.

Cara nodded.

It was early afternoon, but we hadn't eaten since diner leftovers early that morning. The kitchen was fully stocked, a nice touch in a place where, as far as I could tell, they had to have groceries air-dropped in.

Cara made fettuccine Alfredo with canned peas, and it was perfect. We sat at the breakfast nook in the kitchen, not wanting to disturb the place settings in the formal dining room.

"If you will do the cooking," I said around a mouthful, "I will do all the cleaning while we're here. Like, all of it. You're much better at this than me."

"I poured a jar of sauce on some noodles. Not rocket science."

"I've had badly cooked noodles. Trust me. There is a science to it, rocket or not."

"Oh no," Cara said. I looked up, and she shook her head, smiling. "I could've made a video for your grandmother while I cooked. This wouldn't have been good enough anyway. I'll check the pantry later and see if I can come up with something worthy."

I impulsively wiped sauce from her chin with my fingers. "That sounds wonderful," I said. "Double points if it's chocolate."

We ate, happy and relaxed, but at one point, I realized we were sitting at a table for four, two empty chairs beside us. I didn't want to remember all those dinners with Bridget and me, Cara and Lorenzo, but the shadow of those times rose up, just for a moment.

Were they happy? According to Mesmio, they were, but it was easy enough to pretend, in a few minutes of video. I imagined Bridget's smile failing as soon as the camera was off, and it saddened me, unexpectedly.

But I had no reason to think that Lorenzo wasn't making her happy, just because I couldn't.

Still, I didn't want them here at our table. I wanted Cara and this moment all to myself.

I was absolutely stuffed by the time the food was gone. I groaned in happy misery as I cleared the table, discovered a full wine rack in the kitchen, poured Cara and myself full glasses, and started the dishes.

Once the dishwasher was running, I wiped down the countertops and table while Cara watched. She gave the tiniest gasp when I buffed water drops off the faucet.

I looked at her, but she had turned away, cheeks reddening. I suddenly felt motivated to deep clean every room in this house and see if I could get her to moan.

You never can guess a person's kink.

Chapter Twenty-three

There were large spotlight-style flashlights, insect repellant, and a stack of towels by the back door. We helped ourselves, emptying Cara's tote bag of paperback books to carry our supplies, along with some water bottles, her awful granola bar bricks, and the rest of the wine.

Cara and I wore our swimsuits with shorts and shirts on top, both aware of how strong the sun seemed here and how rare the shade in comparison to home.

We walked out the back door and immediately stopped.

Lane's mom had a terraced cactus garden, now in full bloom after the recent rains, with white and yellow and pink blossoms. Some of them lived in beautiful glazed pottery. Some of the flowers were prickly looking themselves, but others just the same as any other spring flower, sprouting soft-looking petals. The cacti themselves were in every shape and size, in dozens of hues of green. I had no idea how many species they represented.

There were rocks, too, boulders really. Granite and what looked like volcanic rock, all arranged amongst the plants, and behind it all, huge yucca and a few palm trees, their wide accordion leaves making a slight rustling sound in the breeze.

In one corner, Lane's mom had a brick firepit and wooden chairs. I'd be willing to bet there were s'mores ingredients in that wonderfully stocked kitchen. That would be a worthy Mesmio reel for Grandma Singh: American-style s'mores.

Lizards darted away from us over the rocky soil as we started down the path between the shrubs and spindly bushes and wild cacti and short, gnarled trees.

The sky was a crystalline blue, the wind warm on my face.

"I thought the desert was just sand," I confessed as I stopped to let a dozen white butterflies cross our path.

"Like the Grand Canyon is a big hole?"

"Yes. I feel like my education has some, well, some really big holes. Are lakes not just water? Is the Arctic not just ice?"

"Really, really not."

I pointed. "Even the rocks are beautiful out here. Layers of red and cream and orange in these amazing formations."

Cara didn't answer. I put a hand on her shoulder.

"It is beautiful here," I said.

She stopped and looked at me, then looked around. "Is it beautiful where we live, too?"

I leaned closer to her. "So beautiful. We have millions of trees, oaks and pines and others, I'm sure, but that's all the tree names I know without making shit up. We have rivers and bayous and botanical gardens. And there are those incredible vines with dark orange flowers that grow up under the overpasses, fifty feet into the air. Have you seen them, Cara?"

She nodded slowly. "I think…I forgot to notice it. Before this week, I hadn't stopped and appreciated anything in a long time."

I wanted to kiss her so badly. I swear, her lips took over ninety percent of my thoughts these days.

But instead, I turned so we were standing side by side, looking out over the landscape together.

I felt the same, in a way, like I'd been caught up in my own thoughts too much to notice the beauty around me, but I suspected that for Cara, it had been much longer than a couple of months. She'd been unhappy for a long time, whereas I had been mostly happy, running my store and living my life in cheery ignorance of the fact that my lying slug of a wife was cheating on me.

Still, I wasn't in a hurry to move from this spot. If I'd tried this with Bridget, if I'd said *Hey let's take a minute and enjoy the view*, she would've rolled her eyes and gone back inside.

I decided a long time ago that I didn't need her to pay attention, that I could enjoy the world without having someone to share my joy, and I was right. But damn, it was nice to share it. It was beyond nice, when Cara noticed the blue outline of the mountains in the distance, to hear her breathing change. It was beyond nice, when she looked down, to watch the toes of her sneakers sift the multicolored stones, knowing that she, like me, was watching how the sunlight glinted off the surfaces and how quickly the dirt darkened as she brushed away the top layer, the ground still wet underneath from the rain.

"I used to read Mary Oliver's poetry every day so I didn't feel alone," I told her, the words bursting out of me like a confession.

"Mary Oliver?"

"Oh, that's right. You're a science nerd. Not a literary nerd."

"Or a music nerd," she said, grinning. "I don't know why it surprises me so much that you're a poetry reader."

"I don't either. Poetry is music. I'll show you later. I brought…a couple of her books with me."

"How many is a couple?" she asked, catching my hesitation.

"All of them," I confessed. "She wrote about paying attention, about nature, about wonder, about being a person in a world that doesn't make it easy."

"The music nerd has hidden depths," she said with a little laugh. "Don't forget, later. I want to see all your favorite poems." Then she took my hand just long enough to pull me forward. "Come on. Hot springs, remember?"

Chapter Twenty-four

Lane was right. We couldn't miss it. There was a single gravel path leading from the back door, through the cactus garden, and out into the desert.

The air smelled clean and earthy, with an almost herbal scent. I bent over some cacti and breathed deeply.

I worried that the day would be too warm for the hot springs to be enjoyable, but when we reached them, half a mile from the house, neither Cara nor I hesitated. We pulled off shirts, shorts, and shoes, left them in a pile on the rocks, and eased ourselves into the clear, warm water.

I wore a plain black one-piece that was advertised as *slimming*, if such a thing can ever be said about two square feet of fabric. Cara's swimsuit was red with orange hibiscus. It was two-piece, and it didn't quite contain the voluptuousness of her ass, the faint tan line separating warm brown and soft-looking paler skin, so I had to restrain both my voice and hands until she was submerged.

Had we never even changed clothes in front of each other on our days of travel? We'd spent so much time rushing from tourist attractions to hotels, taking turns showering and falling asleep quickly. Had I realized how enthralling her curves would be beneath those sundresses and embroidered jeans, I would've paid more attention.

There were several recesses in the rocky ground, some deep, some shallow, some comfortable, some that I'd use to heat up soup but would never get in myself. The whole area smelled faintly of sulfur, but very faintly. The absence of a chlorine smell was actually the strangest part. I rarely swam in lakes or rivers or the ocean. Most of the water I'd touched in my life had been treated with chlorine, whether a little out of the tap or a lot in the city swimming pool.

"Dear goodness," Cara moaned in a way that made my mouth water. She slid down until her shoulders were covered in the warm water, her head resting on the rocky ledge. I forced myself to stop searching for another glimpse of her butt, but dear Lord.

I was not a butt person. I was very much a boob person, if anything, though I'd like to say for the record that all humans are beautiful, and personality matters so much that I'd rather get slapped in the face with a live porcupine than date most of the good-looking people I actually knew in person.

However, I'm also not one to ignore a wonder of the natural world.

I pressed my eyes closed as I tried to stop my brain's obsessive fantasies. What had Cara said? Oh yes, *dear goodness*. Before I could imagine a few other situations that might elicit the phrase, I turned toward her.

"What do you think? Is it worth a ruined vacation in the redwoods?" I asked, slipping a little as I eased myself deeper into the water.

"No," she said, "but all of a sudden, I don't mind as much."

I took her lead and submerged myself up to my chin, letting the heat gently flow over me. When I stopped moving, I could see little fish darting between us.

"How can they swim in this without cooking?" I asked.

Cara watched them, grinning as they darted around us. "They've adapted," she said. "There are even microorganisms in Yellowstone's boiling springs."

I stopped. "Wait, are they really boiling?"

"Not all the time, but yeah, sometimes. All that volcanic activity isn't as far under the surface as you'd think."

I looked around. I don't know what I was checking for. Magma? Smoke? But everything around us was calm. There was only the faintest hint of steam over some of the pools.

For a time, we relaxed in silence, listening to the gentle sounds of the water, the wind rustling bushes and trees, the occasional skittery sound of what I chose to believe were lizards and definitely not snakes or javelinas or giant, hairy scorpions.

Cara's eyes were closed. "I don't know the last time I went somewhere I couldn't even hear cars."

I thought about that, about the people driving in and out of White Sands, even the distant noise of traffic at the Gila cliff dwellings. I snapped my fingers, "Got it. Walking in the pouring rain after your car broke down. Not a car around for miles until Mildred and Jeffrey came along."

Cara nodded. "True, but not exactly a moment to relax and enjoy the nature sounds."

"Hey. Tornadoes and coyote packs make nature sounds, too."

"By that logic, the noise coming out of your mouth would qualify, and I guarantee you, it doesn't."

I laughed but shut up. I didn't know if she was joking, but I was enjoying the quiet, too.

Soon, I got out of the water just long enough to grab the wine and water. I was shivering by the time I got back into the hot spring. I didn't know if the water was that much warmer, or if the day was beginning to cool.

Cara and I passed the wine bottle back and forth. It had a Canada goose on the label, which made me smile, remembering my conversation with my dad about Canadian sweet potatoes in the brownies Mom made. I'd have to make sure to send him pictures of this place. I doubted either of my parents had bothered to download Mesmio.

But he needed to see this. Dad was every bit the comfort traveler. He and Mom had pictures in hammocks on sandy beaches, eating fancy chocolate, and taking trains through beautiful countryside. There were no photos from the tops of any mountains, none that involved trekking through rainforests or sweating more than was absolutely avoidable.

I half suspected that he'd only agreed to attend my college graduation because I'd raved about the foot massage place down the street.

We'd have plenty of opportunities to take pictures and make videos now, I supposed. Cara and I would have several long days of boredom at the vacation house, unless we were going to spend all day every day out here in the hot springs, a plan that sounded good until I noticed the pink tint on the top of Cara's nose. Maybe there were some parasols tucked away in that well-stocked house.

I suddenly regretted not getting the inflatable life-size alien I'd seen in Roswell. It would've made a perfect addition to our hot springs videos.

By the time the wine bottle was empty, the sky had started to take on an orange glow.

"We should head back," Cara said, but she didn't move, her legs stretched out in front of her, the fish darting across her stomach, her bathing suit top thin and clinging.

Dear goodness.

I cleared my throat and tried to focus. The wine wasn't helping. "We have the flashlights," I said. "Let's stay awhile."

It was hard to comprehend how quickly the heat went out of the desert air when the sun began to set. It was like there was no atmosphere to hold it in. The sun was either baking you, or it was gone, and there was nothing, no source of heat but the water. Houston was hot all day and all night. During the worst of summer, it was never below ninety degrees, not even at midnight.

But Houston also had some serious light pollution. Above us now, like a city waking up in the predawn darkness, stars lit up the sky. First, there were a handful. Then, there were more than I had ever seen. And they kept appearing, making the dome of the world feel alive.

The sky next to the shitty motel had nothing on this masterpiece.

I watched them breathlessly, and when I realized Cara hadn't noticed, I pointed overhead, showing her Orion and Cassiopeia, the only two constellations I could regularly find. Even the Big Dipper seemed too sparse in this mess of stars. I kept thinking I'd found it, only to find it again somewhere else.

"It's remarkable that any of those stories are remembered," I said. "So much time has passed, but also, I could find a million shapes up there. I'd find a new one each night, a new story."

"Of course you would," Cara said with a little laugh. "You don't have the kind of mind that can be satisfied with the same old boring story. Even if you told the same one twice, it would be from someone else's perspective. We know what Poseidon thought of Cassiopeia, but what did she think? What did her daughter Andromeda think? By the time you were done, we'd have the whole story."

"Thanks?"

"It's a compliment, believe me. As for me, I'd remember those stars and that they were Cassiopeia, chained to a chair and destined to drown. I'd remember, and pass on the story, and add nothing new."

I wanted to disagree with her, but I wasn't sure how. Maybe Cara didn't see herself as creative, but that was fine. Not everyone was.

But she loved new experiences, even when they scared her. And she had planned out this adventure for us with almost no notice and a very limited budget. And she sang along to the songs on my playlist.

Maybe she wouldn't add to the stories, but they wouldn't be the same without someone like her to clap and laugh and try to understand them in her own way. They wouldn't be the same without her.

I didn't know how to say any of that, so I asked her questions about aliens and how far the planets and stars were and what dark matter was and whether it was real, to which she reliably replied, "I teach biology, not astronomy."

The temperature continued to fall.

I sank lower, covering my chin and lips and breathing through my nose. I was about to say that we should probably go back to the house, when Cara broke the silence.

"Nine years, and he never washed a dish."

I sat up, sure that I'd gotten water in my ears and misheard her. "He what?"

"We'd talk about it. He'd say, what's the big deal? He'd say, why are you getting upset? And nothing would ever change. Eventually I gave up."

She stared out at the night without moving, hardly seeming to breathe.

"It's just one thing. I mean, there were lots more, but it's what I keep thinking about. I told my mom once, and she laughed it off. It's just dishes, after all. I didn't know how to tell her that it was this small thing, but it was every day of my life. Every day, he was saying that his time was more important than mine, that he chose the convenience of a live-in servant over changing this small thing that bothered me. If I'd given it to him, if I'd said I don't mind dishes, just leave them in the sink, then we could've been happy. But it wasn't something I gave. It was something he took from me, just a small piece, every day of my life."

I reached over and took one of her hands, holding tight to it under the water.

She didn't pull away. "Honestly, that was one of the best parts of him cheating on me. Suddenly, he wasn't around after work. I'd cook and eat and clean up, and it made me feel lonely, but that was still better than how he made me feel when he was there."

I didn't move, just listened.

Cara shook her head. "I'm silly. I know."

"No," I said immediately, fiercely. "You're not silly. You're right. You tried to communicate, which is all you could do. He was a shitty partner. That's all."

Tears fell from her eyes, dripping down her cheeks and chin to plop soundlessly in the hot spring.

"Cara, you deserve someone who communicates, too, someone who respects you, and who loves you more than they love themselves. Cara Espinoza…are you listening to me?"

She nodded, and I held her hand until her tears stopped.

"Thank you," she said at last. "Thank you for believing me and not brushing me off."

"Well, you are quite the drama queen."

She gave a soft, wet laugh. "I'm also a compulsive liar."

"Really?"

"No."

I laughed, and after a second, she let go of my hand and pushed me playfully, smiling.

"I can't believe we spent all these years not really being friends," she said. "I mean…"

"I know. Me, too. We could've been hanging out and having fun while Bridget and Lorenzo were being boring."

Cara grinned. "We could've been ditching them and going on adventures, this whole time."

"We could've gone to see the boiling fish in Yellowstone."

Cara seemed like she was about to correct me, then just shook her head. "We can still do that. Barbados, too, like Doug recommended. It was a very good suggestion. And we'll try Muir Woods again, sometime."

"Definitely," I agreed, then bumped her shoulder with mine. "I'm sorry I didn't call you, when I first found out about Bridget and Lorenzo."

"It's okay," Cara said. "I knew. I mean, we found out around the same time, so it didn't make a difference."

"Still. I wish I'd been there for you."

"We weren't that kind of friends then, Honey. But we are now, aren't we?"

I grinned and hugged her, lifting her inches out of the water, squeezing so hard that she squealed, then laughed.

And I…well, I fought to stay on friendship mode and not focus on the feel of her body against mine, the way my hands slid across her wet skin as I reluctantly let her go.

The dream I'd had about us had lingered, deepening into fantasies that were so much more than that. I didn't just want a night with Cara, though I thought about it so much it bordered on meditation. I wanted her friendship, her conversation, her road trips, her morning breath, her bad music. I wanted it all, and I wanted it enough to wait, enough to hope, that someday she'd want it, too.

Chapter Twenty-five

We had taken turns recording each other and the beautiful hot springs throughout the evening. I knew that you could never tell the whole story from what you saw on social media, but as often as we'd done this, taking short bits of video to share our experiences, I never felt like I was faking or acting for the camera. And it seemed like Cara felt the same.

Often enough, it gave me the impetus to say out loud what I was already thinking.

Granted, I didn't often refer to swimming holes as *Cara soup*. But the steam rising over the water had thickened as the sun began to set, and the bowl-like shape that the trickling water had carved out here made a perfect cooking pot.

Cara rolled her eyes when I said it and lifted up a palm full of water, which I drank, pressing my lips to her hand.

"Ew," she said, laughing. "Our feet are in this water."

"Our whole bodies are in this water, and it's the feet that gross you out most?"

Of course, I ended up trying to put my foot in her face after this revelation, and she pretended to gag while trying to escape onto the dry rocks.

I grabbed her, slipped, and landed us both underwater, only saving her phone from the same fate by lifting it straight over my head at the last minute.

I couldn't remember ever feeling so abandonedly happy.

❖

Later, Cara went to pee on some cactus, and I returned a call from the music store that I'd missed.

"Nothing's wrong," Florence said right away. "Except we're down to the last ten ukuleles, which is a good thing. Sold a few guitars this week, too. Just thought you'd like to hear business is hoppin'."

"That is nice to hear," I told her. I was sitting on the edge of the pool with my feet in the warm water. It was my new official favorite way to make phone calls. "Is Doug still singing songs from *The Lion King*?"

"He learned one from *Lilo and Stitch* now. The Hawaiian rollercoaster one. It's been popular. A couple of kids just stopped and stared. One of them dragged their parents inside."

"That's sweet. No grass skirts, though, okay?"

"Oh," Florence said, her voice serious. "I've been on nonstop cultural appropriation watch with that young man. He's bright on some things, but other times, I think his biscuit's not done in the middle."

"Um. Okay. I ordered some ukulele songbooks, but if there are kids interested, I'll try to find some that are made for a younger audience."

"Hush up. You can take care of that next week, Hon," Florence said. "For this week—"

"I know, I know."

"I will say," Florence added, almost in a whisper, "I loved seeing those cave dwellings in your videos. It's sad and wonderful at the same time, seeing them there, but empty."

I smiled. "I thought so, too."

"Maybe I'll take a vacation there, myself, one of these days. Me and the chickens."

I had no idea what that meant. Did she have literal chickens? In any case, it was nice to talk to her about travel plans and not about my emotional state.

"I'll let you go now, Hon," Florence said. "I'd say have fun, but it looks like you've got it covered."

"Thanks, Florence."

I put my phone back outside the splash zone and slid back into the water. I thought about turning on some music, but there was something in the quiet desert sounds that I didn't want to miss.

Cara came back to the pool and slid in next to me.

"Did you get cactus needles in your butt?" I asked.

"No," she said, with the irritated tone that I adored.

"Are you sure? Do you want me to check?"

She rolled her eyes and splashed me.

"Do you think other people come here?" I asked later, kicking my feet slowly in the water.

"I don't know," Cara said. "I'm sure there are other houses nearby."

"It's probably like living right next to a theme park. At first, you want to go all the time because it's close, but after twenty or thirty trips, it gets old."

"Hmm."

"Maybe all the houses here have their own hot springs. They could just be polka-dotted all over the county."

"That sounds like a dream," Cara said.

When she started yawning, I got out and dug through the bag for towels and flashlights, handing her one of each.

We shivered as we tried to dry ourselves well enough for the walk back to the house.

"Next time," she said, "we'll come out early and leave at noon, not at cold-thirty."

"Less talking, more walking," I said, sliding on my shoes and making one last sweep over the rocks and pools with the flashlight. I was sure we'd be back tomorrow, but I hated the thought of littering even short-term in this incredible place. "The path is…"

"Here," Cara said, walking across the rocky outcrop and back. "No, wait."

My heart started racing before my brain caught up. We had both walked all the way around the hot springs, shining those spotlights that brightened so well…but also made the desert around us look colorless.

We couldn't see the gravel path that was so evident on the way here.

"This is ridiculous," Cara said. "Here, shine your light up so I can see where you are, and I'll walk out a little ways."

She headed away from me before I had a chance to argue, but within a minute, she had reappeared on another bank.

"It's just…I…" she managed, then walked away again.

It made me nervous, but I could see her light clearly sweeping the ground, and she didn't walk far.

Her light swung up and pointed around in the distance, hitting me in the face as it passed, but I could've told her that wouldn't help. Half a mile was too far even for these flashlights.

"Cara," I said. I didn't raise my volume at all. The night was still full of crickets, bats chirping, wind rustling every plant, and a distant coyote, but it was plenty quiet enough for my voice to carry.

She stomped back, her voice at a near scream. "I told you we should've gone back. I told you, hours ago. God, what was I thinking? Take a nosedive off a sand dune, Cara! Let's take the elevator, Cara! Come take a closer look at this wild animal, Cara! Why are you even here?"

I almost laughed, but I could tell she was afraid. "I'm here because I want to be," I told her gently.

She collapsed forward, leaning her head against my shoulder.

"Everything will be fine," I said, wrapping my arms around her. "We'll just sleep here."

"Sleep…where?"

I gestured to the ground. "It's probably midnight already. Five or six hours, and there will be daylight, and we'll make our way back easily."

She stepped back from me. My light wasn't shining on her, but I could see her staring at me.

"This isn't a quirky goddamn adventure for Mesmio, Honey. What if there are snakes? No, not what if. There *are* snakes. There are thirteen species of rattlesnake in Arizona. And that's just rattlesnakes. *Thirteen*."

"Then I'll stay awake," I said, my voice calm, as though I could calm her by broadcasting my lack of worry like radio waves.

"What?" she asked, shaking her head as though she truly didn't understand.

"I'll stay awake and keep watch with the light and make sure no snakes or javelinas or desert centipedes come near."

I regretted the comment about desert centipedes instantly. Cara's flashlight went instantly to our feet. There was nothing but a damp area where we had dripped onto the rock.

"You're…you're going to stay up all night and watch out for me?" she asked, her voice full of doubt, almost mocking.

"Yes," I said. "Of course."

I held back the rest of what I wanted to say. Of course I'll watch out for you. Of course I'll protect you. Of course I will do anything, literally anything, Cara, to make sure you're happy and safe. There was nothing I wanted more.

A still, quiet moment passed between us while she turned from staring at her feet to staring at me. Then she bent to set down her flashlight, stood straight, took a step forward, and kissed me.

Chapter Twenty-six

I'm sorry," she said, gasping. "I should've asked."

"I already asked. That implies consent," I said in a rush, hurrying to get her mouth back on mine.

She laughed against my lips.

I made myself pause and pull away. "Why did you say no, before?"

She was breathless, her lips less than an inch from mine, the nearness unbelievably tantalizing, as though I hadn't already tasted her. My craving for her had only grown.

She swallowed. "I thought…I thought you were being impulsive. I thought that once you'd had a chance to think about it, you'd change your mind about me."

"Cara," I whispered, but I couldn't find another word to follow it. I just kissed her more.

I dropped the canvas bag from my shoulder, hearing the crack of the wine bottle as it hit the rocks. It was probably broken. It was empty, at least, but I'd be lint-rolling glass shards out of our clothes for hours. I didn't care.

I wrapped both arms around Cara, and yes, I had been right, so very right, about those lips. They were soft and delicious and so warm they were almost burning. Her tongue touching mine, so gently, then so fiercely, made me instantly so tingly and eager for more that even the very erotic dreams I'd had about her didn't compare. She kissed me with hunger, with fire, as though whatever reservations Cara had had about me were forgotten.

I could offer her a few. I was married and probably about to be bankrupt. I *was* impulsive and incapable of treading lightly. I had barreled my way into Cara's life the same way I'd barreled into Bridget's, focused more on what I wanted than on what was best. For either of us.

But the thought was passing, subsumed by the softness of her skin and the pressure of our bodies.

One of my hands found the damp hair at her neck. I wrapped my fingers in the soft, dark curls, still carrying the warmth of the hot springs.

Our damp swimsuits were cool to the touch, but where my skin touched her skin was all this perfect, soft heat, and I couldn't resist the impulse to pull her a little tighter, to feel her breasts against mine, to feel her hips, her legs.

I wondered if I should stop kissing her so I could breathe properly, but I couldn't make myself do it. I couldn't lose a millimeter that I'd gained here.

Her hands found my bare back, my neck, my hair. She tugged on my purple streak like she'd been dreaming of the moment.

I'd assumed that Cara would be cautious, like in most things, but in this moment, she was powerful. She was a goddess. She was doing what she wanted with her tongue and hands, and I was standing there, panting and elated and desperate for more.

"We have to…we have to stop," I gasped.

"Why?" she asked, her mouth moving to my neck.

"Because…because fucking on the rocks won't be comfortable for either of us."

She laughed with her lips below my ear. It sounded like a purr.

Oh, I was very much going to do whatever she wanted. In fact, I very much wanted to do everything she'd ever wanted, until she fully understood how a lover was supposed to treat their beloved, until she never again settled for anything less.

"Cara." I moaned without meaning to. I wrapped my fingers around the strings of her bikini top but didn't pull until she reached a hand back and made my fingers close tighter, freeing the bows at the neck and back.

Several worshipful epithets came to mind, but my mouth was already back on hers. I'd gotten a glimpse of her breasts in the dim light and needed to fill in the rest of my impression with my palms and fingertips.

There was something about holding the weight of a breast, feeling its gravity, that made the infinite beauty of the universe clear to me. More than mountains, canyons, landforms, and every glimpse of deep space, this soft shape was holy.

I knew that Cara would laugh at me if I told her. I'd tell her anyway. Later.

❖

At some point, we both lost track of our swimsuits. I took Cara's hand and pulled her carefully to the edge of the hot spring.

She sat down, putting her feet back into the warm water. I kneeled on a stone ledge facing her, up to my armpits in the water, and pulled her forward, kissing her from mouth to breasts to stomach.

"Show me what you like," I whispered and followed her instructions to the best of my ability, my palms making small circles over her nipples, my teeth at her neck.

She made no sign of protest when I pulled her hips closer to the edge of the pool and put my face between her thighs, my hands on her ass, moving over skin that I had fantasized over only hours before.

The taste of the warm mineral water on her skin was unlike anything I'd ever experienced. I licked her slowly, thoroughly, leaving no fold untouched. When I finally centered on her clit, she moaned like she had just watched me wash a whole stack of dishes.

I moved one hand up to her breasts, but her hands were already there, fingertips moving across her nipples, her breath fast. I groaned against her skin.

I pressed my mouth between her legs with a passion that surprised even me, flitting my tongue against her slick skin, my body shaking as much as hers, and when she cried out, gripping my hair, shoving me so hard into her that I couldn't breathe, I was nothing but delighted. I pulled her tighter, licked her faster.

I didn't move away until her cries ended and she pulled me up, out of the water, kissing me ferociously.

Her hands found every hungry part of my body, her mouth at my neck, tongue rough against my breasts, fingers running lightly over my back, my thighs, between my legs with the gentlest touch. I pushed her more firmly against me, barely finding a rhythm against her fingers before I was coming, too, so turned on by her sounds and her eagerness that I was lost in seconds.

She joined me in the water, still kissing me, still exploring my body with her hands the same way I touched her, with awe and reverence.

The heat of the springs was even more divine now, our bodies lax and lazy, floating as much as standing in the deep center.

I was so accustomed to saying *I love you* that the words almost escaped me, making me laugh against Cara's mouth.

"What?" Cara asked, pulling back from my laugh or my stillness. I was such a mess of thoughts that I didn't know what to answer.

"Did you ever expect this?" I asked instead, imagining our days together, so very different than what this night had become.

Cara bit her lip, then nodded, and that shocked me.

"Are you kidding?" I asked. "You can't tell me that this is what you had in mind when you invited me on this trip."

"No," she said, laughing. "Definitely not. But to say that I never thought about it? Never imagined it? That would be a lie."

"Are you kidding?" I asked again, not believing her at all. "When?"

"Oh, goodness, for years."

I backed away from her on impulse. I didn't want to upset her. I wasn't upset, but I was shocked.

Cara didn't seem bothered. She cocked her head to the side and looked at me. I could only barely see her in the starlight and the glow of our abandoned flashlights.

"Come on, Honey. You know what you're like."

"Like?" I couldn't find other words. My brain was stuttering.

"Yes," she said, moving slowly toward me. "You're gorgeous." Her tongue flicked against her upper lip.

I huffed. I was overweight and rarely bothered to do more with my face than clean it. My hair was awesome, but that purple streak could only do so much.

"You are," she insisted, still closing the small distance between us. "Not just your body, though definitely your body, you should know. But also you're fun and interesting, and the way you move, God. I know that you're not being intentionally sensual, but you move like someone…like someone who is comfortable with having elbows."

Now I was laughing, letting her finish her approach and touch me again. "Like someone who has elbows?"

"No, like someone who has elbows and is totally okay with it." She laughed, too, and kissed me gently. "I don't. I never know where my elbows should be, or what to do with my hands when I'm standing, or how to sit without drawing attention to my thighs. I've picked out every piece of clothing in my closet with an eye to minimizing my flaws, and I feel like you've done the opposite."

"I do try to maximize my flaws," I said, biting her earlobe. "I have a pair of pants that makes my ass look like a planet."

"No," she said, sounding half amused, half frustrated. "You dress to maximize the things you like about yourself."

I pulled my head back to look at her. "Do I?"

"Yes. The purple shirt that looks like the one mechanics wear, the one that matches your hair, it fits perfectly against your body, like it was tailor-made. Or the one with the music notes that is way too big for you but is somehow exactly perfect. The capri pants that show off the guitar tattoo on your calf. Oh, and that low-cut black top? Your breasts look delicious in that."

"Yeah, I know," I said, and she grinned, pulling me back against her.

I thought about what she said, and about how none of those clothes were ones I'd brought on this trip. I hadn't believed her when she said she'd been noticing me, that she'd imagined us together. But it was hard to dismiss the evidence.

"I almost told you," she said, "days ago, when we were stuck in the elevator. I daydreamed about it, about touching you for the first time, there in the dark."

A shiver ran through my whole body. I had not been a fan of being stuck in that elevator, but I, too, was perfectly happy to daydream about how it could've gone.

She must have felt the shiver. Her lips smiled against my shoulder, then bit me.

"If it helps," I gasped, "I'm totally okay with you having elbows."

"Very helpful," she sighed, but it wasn't an annoyed sigh. I had my teeth on her neck, my hands on the tantalizing sides of her breasts, all I could reach with our bodies pressed together, and she was happily losing track of our conversation.

I couldn't help Cara become more comfortable with being a human. It was hard, most of the time. Maybe I faked being better at it. Maybe I just worried about different things.

But this, making her love how her body felt, that was something I could do, happily.

As for the rest, maybe being cared for, truly cared for, would help a little, in time.

Chapter Twenty-seven

We found our swimsuits, eventually, and slept briefly on the rocks at the edge of the hot spring, warmed by the proximity of the water and each other, pillowing our heads on folded towels.

I had thoroughly checked the area around the springs before we lay down and assured Cara that this spot was as snake-free, scorpion-free, and centipede-free as any place in the middle of the desert could hope to be.

Eventually, she was too tired to stay awake, and she refused to let me watch over her.

"I can't sleep if you don't sleep," she said, passing out almost instantly.

I sat for a few minutes, listening to the night.

I didn't know whether this night with Cara was the start of something or whether it would stand alone, one wonderful memory in a time of my life when everything else in my life was falling apart. Either way, I was grateful. I might lose Strings & Things, but my world was bigger and more interesting than it had been in a long time.

Also, there's nothing like a night of great sex in a hot spring to help the breakup recovery process. I didn't miss Bridget. I had been too angry to miss her. But even the anger was growing more distant. I had better uses for my energy. And my hope.

Soon, I slept, too, and woke to bright sunlight.

I sat up and stretched, looking around just in time to see a gray-brown tail slither out of sight. I didn't know what it was, but I was going to choose to believe it was not one of Arizona's thirteen species of rattlesnake.

Cara was still asleep, mouth wide open, curls tangled.

I would sure as hell not be telling her about that wildlife sighting.

I checked the rest of the area for creepy crawlies, took one long moment of appreciating the feel of her body against me, then woke her gently, and we groggily stood and started making our way down the very visible path back to the house.

We split the barely edible peanut butter granola bars and the last of the water on the way, and it wasn't long before the cactus garden appeared.

Cara opened the door and turned to me in the doorway. "This was perfect."

I laughed. "I'm pretty sure that we just slept on rocks all night."

"No," she said, pulling me close and placing my arms around her waist. "It was perfect. I mean it. That whole night was magical and unbelievably romantic. I will remember and fantasize about kissing you in the hot springs on a regular basis, for the rest of my life. I don't think you understand how amazing you make everything, how much better you make every adventure."

I didn't have anything to say to that. For some reason, tears filled my eyes.

She kissed me before they could fall, then pulled me to the closest bedroom, into bed, and curled her body against mine as we slept.

❖

Lane had left dinner for us in the fridge yesterday, with a note: *Hope you're enjoying the springs. Call if you need anything.*

"Yes, we are," I answered the note out loud, lining up the takeout cartons on the counter.

"Cara! I made lunch," I shouted.

She came in, hair in a towel, and rolled her eyes at the cartons. "You're quite the chef."

"Only the best for you, Care Bear."

She cringed, laughing. "Thanks, Honeybun."

"No problem, Caramel."

"I hate you a little bit."

I laughed out loud. "Good. I'd hate to think that I messed up our friendship with my incredible hot springs skills."

I ran my hand across her lower back, and she gave a delighted shiver.

We ate together at the table, then finally sorted through our luggage, putting everything away in the two nicest bedrooms. Cara arranged all the lotions and makeup bottles that she hadn't bothered to unpack when we were driving somewhere new every day.

I found a bottle of aloe in the cabinet, and we treated each other's mild sunburns, or attempted to. It turned out that putting our hands all over each other made us want to…put our hands all over each other.

We spent the rest of the afternoon in bed, which was much more comfortable than the hot springs, though a bit less adventurous. The absence of snakes really tipped the scales, though.

I could not get over her breasts, and she laughed at how long I could just stare at them adoringly, then take the weight of them in my hands and sigh with pleasure.

"You just don't understand how glorious you are," I said.

"Are you talking to me or my boobs?" she asked.

"*Uhhhh*," I said, then kissed her to get out of answering. She laughed against my mouth.

We took a long nap under the pillowy blankets, only waking when the doorbell rang that evening.

We heard the creak of the door, then Lane, calling out from the doorway. "Dinner!"

"I think you were right," I whispered to Cara. "You should name your firstborn child after them."

"They're my favorite person in the whole world," she muttered.

"Hey," I said, biting her shoulder, but secretly, I felt the same.

Cara and I dressed and went into the living room, both of us looking revealingly disheveled, but Lane just grinned and kept unloading food: chicken-fried steak, burgers, gravy, sweet potato fries, several slices of pie, and a jug of iced tea.

"How many people do you think you're feeding?" Cara asked, laughing.

We talked Lane into staying to eat with us, which didn't take much convincing. I got the impression that it was pretty lonely, being a young queer person in a town this small.

I got out glasses for the tea, and Cara brought plates and silverware to the table, and soon, the only sound was chewing. Lane took out their phone, and in a few seconds, Fiona Apple was singing through the living room speaker system, clear and just loud enough for us to enjoy.

After they'd put away half a chicken-fried steak, Lane brushed off their skirt—it was polka-dots today—and said, "Oh, I meant to tell you. My boss, Alyssa, is driving into Phoenix, day after tomorrow. She said she could give you a ride to the airport."

Cara and I looked at each other across the table.

"How would I get my car back?" Cara asked.

"Oh, I forgot about that," Lane said, smoothing the crumbs from their goatee. "I guess one of you could stay."

Cara turned back to me. I hadn't looked away from her. I was already shaking my head. "Tell your boss thanks," I said, "but we'll wait for Bill to get the car fixed."

"Okey dokey, rum and Coke-y," they said, straight-faced.

Cara and I had to turn our faces away from each other to keep from laughing.

"Hey, how are you liking the hot springs?" Lane asked.

Cara kept her face turned away, but I still saw her cheeks pinken.

"They're wonderful," I answered. "It's hard to believe they're just out there, part of nature."

Lane nodded enthusiastically. "The water actually mixes in with cool groundwater before it reaches the surface. Otherwise, it would be too hot to touch."

"Really?" I guess it shouldn't surprise me that Lane would know all about it. "Did you grow up here?"

"In the town, not in this house, but they're everywhere around here."

"One for every backyard?" Cara asked, smiling at me.

Lane chuckled. "Not exactly, but not too far off, either. You may have noticed there aren't a lot of people here. We don't advertise the hot springs in town, and that's just about the only entertainment you'll find for a hundred miles in any direction."

"You don't advertise?" I asked. "Why?"

Lane shrugged one shoulder. "You ever been to the beach when it was crowded? Or just after a holiday weekend, when there's trash everywhere?"

I nodded, wiping my greasy fingers on a napkin. "Fair point."

"'Course, Mom's the exception, but she's the only one with a vacation rental for miles, and the rental agreement is pretty strongly worded. We don't have many problems."

"I'm sure the diner doesn't mind the extra business when the house has guests," Cara said, snagging the last sweet potato fry.

"That's the truth," Lane said. "But we get plenty of truckers and travelers passing through. It's a small town, but it's a pretty big road."

"And there are some pretty big cities at the end of it," I said. "Do you ever go?"

"Now and then, but most people who grow up here, they either hate it like anything and never come back, or they love it too much to go." At the last, they pointed at themself. "Cities can be lonely when you're used to knowing everyone in town by name."

"That makes sense," Cara said.

"Don't get me wrong—some days I'd commit a felony for a Starbucks Frappuccino, but most of the time, I'm happy."

I had to stop eating and look at them. *Most of the time, I'm happy.*

My dad had said the same thing last week, on the phone. *I'm generally a cheery guy, don't you know?*

Even Florence with her dubious Southern charm: *I'm happier than a dog with two dicks.*

How wonderful, to feel like I was returning to that, after months of dwelling on my own misery.

I pulled a slice of lemon meringue pie over to myself and spooned out some of the lemon filling. It was tart and cold and perfect. I took another spoonful and held it out for Cara to share.

❖

I got out my guitar after Lane left, strumming with very poor posture on the living room couch, singing softly along, a tune and a handful of words that had been percolating in my thoughts.

After a few minutes, I had a melody and some words hashed out. "How did I live so many years without adventure, boxed in and more alone than I knew? How did I live without the adventure of knowing you?"

When I had fiddled with the key and made some notes on my phone, I looked up to find Cara holding hers up, recording me. She was smiling, but her eyes looked ready to overflow.

After a moment, she lowered it. "I won't post it if you don't want me to."

I shook my head. "It's good for the kids to see that you can love music without being Joan Jett."

She laughed, shaking her head. "The kids don't know who Joan Jett is."

"I know!" I groaned, leaning back into the couch cushions. "It's a tragedy."

"Even I can agree with that." She plopped down beside me.

"So what do you think?" I asked. "Do I need some Elton John glasses? Would they make me sexier?"

Cara looked at me, then lifted her hands, making circles with her fingers around my eyes to simulate glasses.

"You'd look ridiculous," she said, seriously.

"Agreed."

"I don't like Kool-Aid, but what about blue lipstick instead of red?" She made a kissy face.

"I'd actually like to see you in every shade of every color. Is that strange? I want to find just the right one to bring out the gold in your eyes, and then—"

She kissed me, slow and soft, touching my cheek and then running her fingers over and through my hair, murmuring, "So soft," in between kisses.

After a few minutes, she sat back. "I'm sorry. You were saying?"

I laughed. "I was about to say that I wanted to paint your lips rainbow colors, then have you kiss me on the cheek because that would look really cool."

Cara pinched me. "Such a romantic."

CHAPTER TWENTY-EIGHT

I made bacon and eggs for breakfast, my specialty. Cara ate two helpings and told me that I was beautiful.

She insisted on helping clean up, even though I cooked. I let her dry the dishes as I finished washing them, then put a dollop of bubbles on her nose, which somehow evolved into foreplay.

Cara had just said, "We should walk to the springs before it gets too hot," when my phone rang.

"Now, I don't want you to worry. Everything is fine," Mom said, which is probably the least comforting thing anyone had ever said to me.

"What is going on?" I asked, moving away from Cara, who looked concerned at the sound of my voice.

Suddenly, every sound and movement in the house was too distracting. I went outside.

Mom went on with her forced-calm voice, "Badger had a little seizure. He—"

"A little seizure! What is a little seizure?" I closed the door and sat on the nearest rock.

"It's okay, Honey. We're at the vet now, and they're doing a full workup. I wasn't even sure if I should tell you until we had the results because it just happened once, and Badger is doing just fine now."

Her voice didn't waver from its calmness, and that somehow made me angrier. "Obviously, he is not fine. What did they say? What could've happened? Did he get hurt? Did he hit his head?"

"No. He was with me in the garden all morning. I checked him for ticks, for bites, anything I could think of. Some dogs just have seizures, so there may not be a cause, but if there is, Dr. Bob will find it."

I stood there, berating myself for trusting my beloved Badger to the care of someone named Dr. Bob, and more than that, for leaving. What if Badger was really sick? What if he needed me, and I wasn't there? God, what if he died?

I took a breath and held it. I wanted to scream at Mom, but I'd spent my teen years doing that, and I'd promised us both that I was done behaving like a child. And even while my heart was racing and my stomach turning, I knew that she wouldn't let Badger come to harm any more than she would me, if she had the power to stop it.

"Honey?" Mom asked. "Do you want to stay on the phone, or do you want me to call you when there's news?"

I didn't know. What I wanted was to be there, to be the one demanding answers from the vet, to be holding Badger. I imagined him there, shaking with a seizure, not knowing what was happening.

"Honey? I…oh wait, here he is now." Mom spoke to the vet, and then I heard the noise increase as she switched to speakerphone.

"Go ahead," she told him.

"Hello, Ms. Singh. Badger is doing well now. His toxicology labs came back with one alarming sign, which is good, actually. It means there's no serious injury. Badger just needs to stay away from onions."

"Onions?" I asked, while Mom gasped.

"Onions! Oh my Lord, he was digging in last year's onion bed. I didn't even realize. Oh, Honey, I'm so sorry. This is all my fault."

Dr. Bob went on, "It's nothing you could've known to look out for. Not a lot of dogs will ingest onions on purpose. Certainly not raw. And most will have only a slight stomach upset, if anything. Badger just seems to be particularly sensitive to the chemicals in onions, and particularly attracted to them. It's unfortunate, but it's the way it goes sometimes."

"But he'll be okay?" Mom asked, sounding teary.

"He's just fine. You can take him home now. Just make sure he gets plenty of water, and keep him inside as much as you can."

There was another shift in the sound levels as Mom turned off speakerphone.

"Honey," she said.

"It's okay, Mom. You heard him. There is no way you could've known that Badger has a self-destructive love of onions."

I was half laughing, half crying.

Mom must have held the phone close to Badger. I could hear his happy panting breaths.

"I love you, you little jerk," I told him.

When I went back inside, Cara was waiting, still and wide-eyed.

"I'm sorry. I didn't mean to freak you out," I said. "My dog had a seizure."

Cara put both hands over her mouth. "Badger? Is he okay?"

I smiled and let out a breath that I felt all throughout my body. "Yeah. He's fine."

We got a later start back to the hot springs than we'd planned, but we hurried into our still damp swimsuits and left the house by nine a.m. Cara had even found a portable patio umbrella stand and bright pink umbrella, so we could have some shade. It had a strap, so I slung it over my shoulder for the walk down the trail.

Halfway there, I took her hand.

"You can go, if you need to," she said after a while.

"Go where?"

"Home. If you want to take Lane's boss's offer and fly home on that rickety airline or whatever." She shrugged. "I'd understand."

"Very tempting," I said with a laugh. "But no. All I want is more days here with you."

I tried to feel as sincere as I sounded. I did want to get home to see Badger. I ached to see his ugly little face for myself and know he was okay.

But there was also a lot that I had to do when I got home, and if I could just have a few more days, a few more days of not opening the letter on my desk, a few more days of ignoring my problems before I became a divorcee and a failed business owner. And probably homeless.

But for the first time, the thought didn't entirely overwhelm me. Cara had been right about how different the world seemed, how much bigger, after this trip. Or I guess, this half of a trip.

If I had to, I could find another path for myself. There were plenty of them in the world, just waiting.

For a moment, I let myself imagine them. I could go back to school and study something new. I could sell whatever I had left and travel until my money was gone. I could look for jobs overseas.

It was easy, even in a place as huge as Houston, to let the world shrink down to the places you'd already been, the people you'd already met. But there was more out there. So much more.

Our trail ended at the quiet clearing, the only sound the wind, the surface of the water emitting its familiar mineral scent.

"God, it's lovely here," Cara said, and all my muscles began to relax. Sometimes you needed someone to remind you, someone like Mary Oliver to say *Stop and see*.

Cara immediately wiggled out of her shorts and T-shirt and sandals and put her feet in the water. I watched her, enjoying every expression, every soft, happy sound.

She slid down fully into the water.

"Did you see the projector in the living room?" I asked. "We should watch a movie later. I bet there's popcorn in the pantry."

"Mmm," Cara said, sinking down to her chin.

"It's hard to have a conversation with you when you're this relaxed," I mock complained.

"Mmm, partly your fault," she muttered, eyes closed.

I grinned and went to set up the umbrella.

We spent an hour floating, soaking, moving in and out of the umbrella's shade. I didn't want to rush her or to assume, but when she finally reached out to pull me to her, I was giddy. I bit her earlobe, her neck, her shoulder, licking the hot water off her skin.

Cara reciprocated. Soon, we were both hungry and panting, hands and mouths desperate.

"Wait," I gasped, tugging at the clasp on the back of my swimsuit.

"I can't. I have no patience when it comes to you," Cara said. She pushed me onto the lip of the pool, shoving aside clothes and licking my breasts, my nipples, and when she lowered her head between my legs, I was gone in an instant, not holding back the near scream that emerged as my body shook under the hot desert sun.

CHAPTER TWENTY-NINE

It was probably a bad choice, a movie about a breakup, even a funny one. Cara and I laughed, sometimes at the wrong parts, but at least we laughed.

I kissed her throughout one sexy scene, the actors' moans merging with ours.

By the midpoint, it was clear that the characters' relationship was heading for disaster. I made some popcorn, and Cara curled against me when I returned to the couch.

A familiar actor played the psychologist, and Cara and I tried to place her, eventually giving up on our guesses and searching our phones for the answer. We were wrong on every guess.

"Bridget and I never tried that," I said at one point, gesturing to the screen with a handful of popcorn. "It was too fast, I guess. I only knew there was a problem when she left."

Cara was quiet for a minute, then said, softly, "We tried it. Marriage counseling."

I glanced at her out of the corner of my eye, my attention still mostly on the movie. "I didn't know that."

Cara gave a little shrug, a little head shake. "It didn't do us much good. Our last was right around Valentine's Day. We were in a session when Lorenzo told me that he was filing for a divorce."

I nodded. We'd talked about this. Bridget had let me know around the same time. We hadn't been in counseling. She'd just told me on the way out the door one Sunday morning. By the way, I'm leaving you. By the way, I don't love you anymore. By the way, I've been sleeping with someone else because I'm a lying, cheating slime of a human being who has been lusting after my best friend for years.

Maybe if I'd known, if we'd tried counseling, too. Maybe if we'd tried it long ago, before Bridget had one foot out the door. Maybe it would've mattered.

"How long had you been in counseling?" I asked.

"Since…a few months." She glanced at me, then away.

There was something about it, about the timing, about her expression, about the hesitation in her answer that itched at my thoughts.

I shook my head and tried to pay attention to the movie, but the itch remained.

Couples went to counseling for lots of reasons. Obviously, there were problems in their marriage. Every marriage has problems.

But…

I almost didn't ask. I almost decided that I was being paranoid, that I was letting the hurt and the anger make me suspicious even when there was no reason.

But Cara still wasn't looking at me, and she wasn't watching the movie, either. She was staring at her clenched hands.

"Did you start counseling," I asked slowly, "before or after he and Bridget got together?"

Cara's sunburned face lost some of its color.

It was something I'd wondered about, in the back of my mind. I knew that I worked late in the music store, and Bridget and I had frequent rocky spells. This one had been particularly long. But she was always there when I got home. It hadn't occurred to me that she would cheat. I had been caught unawares, unpleasantly surprised.

But Cara hadn't been. Cara left school after teaching all day and went home and her husband wasn't there, day after day.

She ate dinner alone. She'd said that she rarely saw him at all. Surely, he'd given her some believable excuse. He was working. He was hanging out with friends.

I watched her mouth, her eyes, her hands curled into fists.

She was alone, she'd said. Day after day.

"After," she admitted, meeting my eyes. The word gutted me.

"You knew," I said, trying to force the words out, but suddenly, I had no air. "You knew they were together."

Cara's head shook slightly, but it wasn't a denial. She had tears in her eyes, and her voice trembled. "The counseling was helping.

We were having conversations that we'd been putting off for ages. I thought…I thought maybe…"

"How long did you know?" I went from staring at her to not being able to look at her at all.

"Months," she said.

I tried to breathe through the nausea. Months? Months? "You didn't tell me," I accused. "Months, and you didn't tell me."

I stood and paced the living room, clenching my hands together to stop the trembling.

When she'd come into the store that first day, she'd looked demolished. She'd asked, first thing, if I'd known about Bridget and Lorenzo, and I'd been so wrapped up in how *I'd* been betrayed, how angry *I* felt, that I hadn't even returned the question.

Because of course I hadn't known. If I'd known, I would've been a decent human being and told her.

I put my shaking hands over my face.

And I'd felt *guilty*. Going to her apartment to apologize for being an ass, I'd regretted not reaching out to her after Lorenzo and Bridget left us. I'd sat at her table, commiserating like she was just another abandoned spouse. I'd apologized to her for not calling.

I had apologized. And all that time, she'd been part of it, part of keeping the secret, part of keeping me in the dark.

All that time. All that time on the road, all those days and nights together, being more open with her than anyone since Bridget, maybe even including the years I spent with Bridget, and Cara had listened and never said a word.

I forced my hands down to my stomach and wrapped my arms around myself, turning to face her. "Why?"

Cara gave one soft gasp, almost a sob, then whispered, "As long as your marriage stayed in one piece, there was a chance mine would, too."

I walked across the room, unable to be near her. "What are you talking about?"

"If you knew they were together," she explained, tears running down her cheeks that I wanted to kiss away, even now with anger rising up so strong in me that I could feel it in my throat, "if you knew, then you and Bridget would split up. Bridget would be free to be with

Lorenzo. Then…then there would be no reason for him to stay with me."

I tried to listen and to process her words.

She went on, "It's all I had, that chance that Bridget would decide to fix her marriage. Lorenzo didn't care about his." Tears ran down her face. "You don't have to tell me it's pathetic. I know."

"Pathetic," I murmured, but it wasn't agreement or disagreement, just a word among a hundred words that made little sense to me at the moment.

"Yeah," she agreed. "I didn't want to face what was happening to me, but I should…I should've—"

I shook my head, holding up a hand for her to stop, but I was surprised when she actually did. I looked at her, this unbelievably sexy and funny and lovable woman, tears running down her face, her eyes wide and sad.

I'm sorry, I'd said to her, that day in her kitchen, out of sympathy for the collapse of our marriages, our plans, what had felt, at the moment, like our lives.

I'm sorry, too, she'd said.

And maybe she had been. Maybe she was now. But last night, I'd held on to her as though our lives were starting over again, and she had still been lying.

I felt temporarily zapped of emotion, as though my brain had overloaded and needed to cool down and restart.

"I…I'm going for a walk." I was impressed with how calm I sounded.

"Honey," she said as I slid my feet into my shoes and walked out the back door.

I didn't stop.

I started walking down the path to the hot springs, then turned back, disgusted. I walked around the house instead, heading down the gravel road.

I wanted to think about what Cara had said, and at the same time, I never wanted to relive that conversation, ever again.

Cara had let me believe that my marriage was fine, that my wife wasn't sleeping with anyone but me, when I'd been sharing her for months.

I stopped and threw up in some tall grass at the side of the road.

All I could see was my past self, standing behind the register at work, while somewhere Bridget was off fucking Lorenzo, and Cara was at home *knowing*.

Home…by herself, which meant that Bridget and Lorenzo had probably been at my house, in our bed, next to the picture of the two of us on our wedding day, me in my beautiful purple dress, Bridget beaming, radiant in blush and tulle.

I'd never thought to wonder before where, exactly, my wife was located when she was fucking someone else. I'd have brushed it off as a minor detail, maybe because it wouldn't have occurred to me that she was getting dick in our bed.

Not the couch. No, that would be way too uncomfortable, and Bridget was all about the comfort. No floor or shower or dining room table sex for her. She needed a mattress with a memory foam topper.

Though, what did I know? Maybe if there were testicles in the equation, she'd be happy on the floor.

I shook my head at my own pettiness. Besides, testicles didn't have the power to change someone's nature.

Weirdly, I thought of Tamara and her blue Kool-Aid lips, how I'd adored her for so long, obsessed with her, and how she'd turned out to be someone completely different than the person I thought she was.

Could I even trust my own observations? Did I see people wrong? Or was everyone but me so good at hiding their true selves that they could pretend, for years, until one day it was just too exhausting to fake it?

I didn't know if I believed any of that, or I wanted to believe it, even if it was true.

I thought of my parents, who were complex and sometimes contradictory, but who were always their true selves, even when I was a teenager and their true selves pissed me off daily.

And me? Was I always out there, for everyone, never pretending? I spent a lot of days working retail, so no, that wasn't entirely the case. But with my friends, my family, people I cared about and respected? Yes. I didn't pretend. I wasn't even sure I knew how.

I kneeled and wiped the sweat and tears from my face with my T-shirt before covering my eyes with my hands and trying to breathe. I kept gasping, and it took effort to pull air all the way in and push it all the way out.

I did it a few more times, then stood and kept walking.

Okay.

My thoughts had derailed, and I let them. I was used to being mad at Bridget. This was just one more drop in the bucket.

I wasn't used to being mad at Cara, and I was surprised by the sharpness of the pain and how deep it went.

I don't know how long I walked or how far. I tried to tell myself that I was overreacting, and in the next moment, tried to convince myself that I was underreacting. I wanted a drink and sleep and my guitar, and most of all, I wanted to rewind to an hour ago and just be happy.

I'd been happy with Cara. This whole trip had been fun, but the last twenty-four hours had been more than that. We'd had one truly incredible day together.

But it had just been one day.

And now?

Now I wanted to be with my goddamned stupid dog.

Eventually, I realized my phone was in my pocket. I didn't have a strong signal, but I had one. Just enough.

I held my finger over the call button for a full thirty seconds before I pressed it.

"Lane," I said, as soon as they answered. "When is your boss going to Phoenix? I need a ride."

CHAPTER THIRTY

I was glad not to be in Cara's car. It was bad enough to look over and see an empty seat where she should be.

Lane's boss, Alyssa, had been more than happy to give me a ride, though her front passenger seat was stacked with boxes that had to have the AC, or her makeup samples would melt, so I sat in the sweltering back seat.

"It's like I'm your Uber driver," Alyssa joked.

As it turned out, though, she was more like a very bad stand-up comedian in a room in which I was trapped for three hours. She would give me every detail of extremely boring anecdotes, then laugh loudly as though what she'd said had been funny.

Without meaning to, I started imagining how I'd tell Cara about her, mimicking Alyssa's story about buying a lawn mower, and how she'd tracked down a print copy of a *Consumer Reports* about lawn mowers and studied it thoroughly, only to find out it was ten years old and the mowers she read about *weren't even being sold anymore*. Ha ha ha!

I felt a little bad making fun of her, even mentally. She'd been kind enough to drive me and even turned down my offer to pay for gas.

But mostly, I just wanted quiet. I wanted to stop trying to overthink every single choice I made and remember all the good moments of Cara's and my time together, every stop, every remarkable view, to imprint our trip on my mind forever.

I had never done anything like this, this weeklong road trip into the unknown. I'd never seen so many amazing things, learned so much, and talked so much with another human being. I wondered about her road trip questions, whether she'd really just meant to pass the time or because she'd wanted for us to know each other better, whether she'd ever imagined that us getting to know each other would mean caring more than we'd ever expected.

The drive felt longer than any day I'd spent in the car with Cara. I drifted off to sleep at one point and woke up, reaching for her.

Eventually, I saw the airport signs, and Alyssa dropped me at departures, smiling and waving as I struggled with my guitar and suitcase.

The flight from Phoenix to Houston was worse than I imagined. The sterile gray of the airport and plane was like eating paste after the holy natural loveliness of the hot springs. There were too many people, with all their terrible people smells. I paid too much for bad coffee and sat in uncomfortable chairs, wallowing in the wrongness of being here, when Cara and the beautiful world were out there, reachable, but abandoned.

The flight itself was fine. I didn't stress about air travel, even with all the malfunctions in the news. It was possible that the idea of falling out of the sky seemed like the solution to pretty much all my problems.

But when we landed safely in Houston, I had to start facing them.

I got a rideshare, a real one and not a trapped-with-a-comedian nightmare, to Cara's apartment building to get my car. The rideshare's GPS did not sound like Sir David Attenborough. It was such a terrible, boring voice that I could barely stand it.

I stood outside Cara's apartment for a moment, strangely tempted to knock, even though I knew she wasn't there.

Then I got in my own empty car and drove straight to Strings & Things.

The cash register and the bell over the door chimed simultaneously as I entered. Doug was behind the counter and did a double take when he saw me but quickly returned his attention to the customer, who had just bought one of our nicer acoustic guitars.

I looked around. There were customers here. Real customers, some of them putting accessories into our seldom-used handheld shopping baskets.

Florence emerged from the back, looking frazzled, and walked right past me to a waiting customer.

I took a step closer to eavesdrop.

"…will be in tomorrow's shipment, so you'll get the first pick of the Stentor violins."

The customer left empty-handed, but smiling.

"What is going on?" I whispered behind Florence.

She spun around, wide-eyed. "Honey! You're back! Oh no. You're back. What happened?"

"Car broke down. There are *customers* here." It was more a question than a statement, and Florence gestured for me to join her in my office.

The desk looked more organized than I'd left it. I had a sneaking suspicion that the whole business would've run better from the start if Florence had been in charge, though back then she hadn't known a Fender from a Hoover.

I sat in my chair, and she collapsed in the one across from me, looking exhausted.

"At this rate, we'll have to hire more staff. I've been running all over hell's half acre. I can't spend ten hours a day on my feet like I used to."

"More staff?" I gaped. "When I left, I was worried how I was going to keep paying the two that I have. What is going on?"

Her forehead furrowed. "You know."

"I know…what?"

"The Mesmio thing. Your friend posted videos of you playing a couple of times, talking about the store, and of course, the two of you are just adorable anyway."

I tried not to linger on that last part. "What about Mesmio?"

Florence's eyes went wide. "You don't know? You're…what's the word…*virus*?"

It took me a second. "Viral?"

"That's the one, darlin'. We've got people driving in from Katy, Friendswood, Baytown, the whole area. Doug got the idea to ask them to post about the store online, even got a couple of funny signs made up—*Don't get strung along. Shop Strings & Things.* He's as smart as all get out. And don't get me started on the online orders."

I was shaking my head. "We've never had a single online order."

"Well, now we do. Doug saved little pictures of you and your friend off the Mesmio, and he writes a note and sends them along with the package. He really is a gem."

My head was whirling. I leaned into the top of the desk for a moment. I focused on Doug forging my signature on notes to my… fans? That should probably stop. But it was a smart idea.

I sat up straight, meeting Florence's worried expression. "Thank you for taking care of everything this week. You have no idea how wonderful it was to get away for a while. I didn't expect to come home to a thriving business, but you know what? We deserve this, you and me and Doug. We've worked hard to get this far."

She smiled, looking relieved. "I better get back out there before they overrun Doug."

She left, closing the door behind her, and I looked at the corner of my desk, at the envelope with my name and address in too-large letters, right where I'd left it.

I picked it up and held it in my hands, feeling the weight of the pages.

A week ago, I had been too afraid to open it, too afraid to acknowledge that my marriage was over, that the woman I'd loved so completely didn't love me anymore.

And I made myself a promise, one that I thought would make Cara proud: I was going to open this envelope, right now, and the next phase in my life was going to begin, and I was going to face it. No, I was going to embrace it.

Bridget was gone, and I truly didn't want her back. My marriage was over, and that felt like a different sort of grief, somehow. But I would grieve while moving forward.

And if Bridget took everything, if she took the store, which she had every right to do, then that would still not stop me. I would make the life I wanted.

And if I failed, I'd know that I did everything I could possibly do to succeed. I would be brave. And I would keep going.

I grabbed a corner and tore open the envelope.

Chapter Thirty-one

Petition for Divorce.

I made myself breathe slowly out and in.

There were a lot of pages, a lot of words, little yellow tabby things to show me where to sign.

I skimmed each page, signing as I went, until…

There it was.

Bridget was taking the house. But she was giving me the store.

I let out a breath that I'd swear I'd been holding for weeks. I had been so sure that she would ask for it all, and what could I have done? My financial contributions had been tiny, compared to hers. She had paid for more than three-quarters of the store.

She could've taken it, the building, the inventory, everything, or demanded that we sell it and split the money. She probably should've. There would be no return on her investment now.

So why hadn't she?

I sat staring at the papers for ages, while the question turned in my head. I could only come up with one explanation.

Bridget had loved me.

How strange, to doubt it so completely for so long and to discover the truth buried in a stack of legal papers.

I remembered the first time we'd come inside this empty building, how her eyes had lit up as she talked about what we should do, what colors to paint the walls, how to arrange the shelving, where to put the register. She'd always had a good eye for design, and I loved how the store had turned out with her help.

I remembered, years before, when she would watch me sing in the evenings, my bare fingers on the strings, her eyes adoring.

I remembered her briefly trying to learn how to play, too. It lasted until her first blister. I brought her an ice pack, assuring her that it was just part of the process. She had stared at me and said, "Why would you do this to me? To yourself? Do you love pain, or are your fingers made of rocks? I'm switching to drums." And I'd laughed. Later, I'd taken her to a friend's house, and she had spent an hour playing on his drum set, headbanging like an eighties rocker.

I remembered putting a ring on her finger and pulling her close to me, amazed that she said yes.

In my office, I wiped the tears from my face, but I was smiling, too, feeling lighter than I had in months.

All those memories that had felt tainted were returning now, bright and new, not because Bridget had left me the store, but because of what it meant. She hadn't spent the last fourteen years lying to me. She had loved me. She'd wanted to be with me. Our marriage had been real and good and wonderful, for years and years.

Of course, I was still angry with her. She'd walked out on me.

But at least she'd done it fast, ripping-off-the-bandage fast. She hadn't let me linger in hope, gone with me to therapy, let me try to make amends once she knew what she wanted.

The fact that *Lorenzo* was what she wanted still baffled me and probably always would.

But I could look at our shared past without flinching now, and that was something.

I did my best to dry my eyes with my sleeve and get back to the paperwork. I picked up the page, starting back at the top and skimming it again.

Bridget also…oh. I dropped the page. It fluttered to the floor, and I had to stoop to pick it up again.

She wanted to split the contents of all our accounts. Fifty-fifty.

I only ever dealt with the business account and our shared checking account, for bills. I'd known she was putting money in savings, but I'd never bothered to check how much. To be honest, I'd kind of forgotten it existed.

And now, now along with the store, I had twenty thousand dollars to help keep it running.

❖

Once I was finished freaking out, I called Mom to check on Badger and let her know that I was back in town.

"Now," she said, "I'm sure you're worn out, so don't worry about coming to get him right away. Are you at the store? I knew you would be. Go home and get some rest. You can pick Badger up in a day or two, once you've recovered from all that travel."

"I'll be there in ten minutes," I told her.

"Figures."

It took me fifteen, but as soon as I pulled into the driveway, Mom opened the door, Badger in her arms.

I took him and buried my face in his fur as he yipped and licked me in my ear.

"Gross," I said, kissing him. He was fine. He was healthy. It didn't even seem like he'd lost an ounce of weight or fur from his ordeal in the onion patch. I squeezed him too tight as I walked inside, then set him down as Dad approached.

"Oh my Honey," Dad said, squeezing me almost as tightly as I'd squeezed Badger. "I'm so glad you're back. I'm glad you went, but your mother had to hide my keys when I saw your video about being stranded in the desert."

"Yes, at that horrible little cottage next to those horrible hot springs," Mom said, grinning.

"That Cara looks like she thinks the world of you," Dad said. "She keeps looking at you like she thinks you're Taylor Swift."

"She's sweet," Mom said, in a tone like she was defending Cara from being called a fangirl. "I know I made a fuss, but it's been wonderful, seeing you so happy. I was wrong, and I'm glad."

I had honestly doubted that they'd kept watching the Mesmio reels, remembering that I'd avoided talking to them about our car trouble when we were on the phone. I was surprised that they hadn't been calling every five minutes to offer to come get me.

Were they treating me like a real adult? Finally?

"The hot springs were beautiful, but I did feel so bad for you both when the car broke down before you got to the redwoods," Mom said.

"She's been obsessing over your Mesmio like it's a soap opera," Dad teased. "But in all seriousness, we *were* worried. Are you okay?"

"I'm so traumatized that I may need another vacation." I tried to joke, but with both of them here chattering, and Badger rolling against my ankles, every hard thing I'd faced in the last few days seemed to hit me all at once, and I felt my eyes start to fill.

I tried to swallow back the tears. I couldn't have even said what I was crying about, and I probably would've stopped, but Mom noticed and put her arms around me.

Then there was no way I could stop. So much for being a grown-up. I leaned into my mommy.

She and Dad hugged me from either side, and I tried to let go of everything I'd been carrying. But there was too much. There was still Cara, who I'd abandoned, who'd lied to me about my own marriage. There was the stress of worry over Badger. There was the store, rescued from the brink of bankruptcy, and mine, truly mine.

I cried over every good and bad and hard thing, every change that had come, and all the challenges still ahead of me.

And for a moment, I tried to look at it all the way I'd looked at the canyon, at the stars, at the sands, the way Mary Oliver would, as something vast and unique, something pushing the boundary of the word *beautiful* to make it bigger, make it encompass more.

Because if I couldn't see my own life that way, what was the point of any adventure?

Eventually, I pulled myself together as much as I could and told my parents the lie that they'd probably told me often, growing up.

"I'm just tired," I said. "It's been a long day, and I'm sure all I need is some rest."

I rejected my mother's pleas to stay in my old room, told them I'd call tomorrow, and took Badger home.

Just inside the front door of my house, I hugged him close to me again, then put him down, letting him run around with joy and bounce against my legs only to run around again and again.

It was wonderful to be home again, almost as much as it hurt. I went straight for the wine.

Badger sniffed corners and jumped up on all the furniture, barked at a plant, then rolled onto my feet, begging for belly rubs.

"You're a pest," I told him. "But I don't know how I could've faced this without you."

Chapter Thirty-two

I spent the next three days with my head in the store's books, planning. We were going to be in the black this month, for the first time ever. I wanted to recklessly double Florence's and Doug's salaries, but I knew what a blow it would be to them if I couldn't keep it going. I settled on a one-time bonus, a thousand each for now, until we saw how long our luck would last.

And every time I took a break, I opened Mesmio.

Bridget and Lorenzo had returned from their cruise, their hair lighter, their skin darker, but that elation I'd seen in her earlier videos was still there. They looked into each other's eyes, even while speaking to the camera. They touched constantly, as though afraid to find that they'd imagined it all, as though confirming that they were both there, together, every moment.

I wondered, not for the first time, how long they had loved each other.

Then I switched over to the videos of buff women chopping logs, as a palate cleanser.

But mostly, I watched Cara's reels.

I hadn't seen all the videos, even the ones she posted while we were traveling together. Others, I'd seen in their original versions, but Cara had edited and uploaded them, so I'd never watched the final product. She was good at video editing, probably better than she realized.

I started at the beginning and watched through to the end.

There we were, chatting together around the alien autopsy table and confiding in the bow-tied alien bartender. Then Cara was filming herself as she gleefully sledded down hills of white sand. Then we were together on the dunes, pointing out the mountains in the distance. We walked through the cliff dwellings. We shared the Grand Canyon. She had even taken a short clip of us, stuck in an elevator, talking about outrunning scorpions, our voices echoing. There were diners and hotel rooms and so many clips of us being ridiculous in the car. There were Mildred and Jeffrey, Mechanic Bill, and a video we'd taken with Lane just a couple of days before. I'd already forgotten. There was me, with my guitar. And there were the two of us at the hot springs, the incomparable beauty of the desert around us.

There were dozens of Mesmio reels, more than I could've imagined.

And then, of course, there were the new ones.

Cara sat in the cactus garden. Her eyes were swollen and teary, like when she'd come into my store just last week and asked me if I had known that her husband was cheating.

I hadn't. She had, but it hadn't crushed her any less. I knew that.

Now, she looked straight into the camera. "It looks like I'll be finishing this adventure on my own. And it's my fault, so keep that in mind when you comment."

She turned the camera to show the cacti, like a terraced garden, in pots of varying heights around those in-ground. She showed a few of the blooms up close, even catching a glimpse of a hummingbird hovering over a blossom, and then there was her face, a little calmer than it had seemed before. It was seconds in Mesmio time, but it could've been hours later.

She smiled. "The world is still beautiful."

In the next video, she and Lane were standing outside the house, holding her luggage.

"I couldn't believe it when I got the call," she exclaimed. "Mechanic Bill is my favorite person in the world."

"Hey," Lane said, jovially, with a shoulder bump.

"Aww, you can be my second favorite," she said. Then, to the camera, "Lane has been my hero more than once over the past few days. First, they let us stay in this beautiful home. Second, they fed us so much and so well that I may have to drive all the way back here sometime soon for the diner's divine chicken-fried steak. And third"—here she stopped to take Lane's arm in hers—"Lane has been a true friend when I needed one. When I was a blubbing fountain of emotion, they brought me ice cream and listened to me whine, and I will be grateful forever."

Lane said, "Aww. And Cara doesn't know this yet, but I'm taking her up on her invitation to visit Houston this summer."

Cara squealed.

Lane laughed and hugged her.

In the next, Cara was back with her orange car, grinning and doing a little dance in the repair shop's parking lot. I caught a glimpse of the awful motel in the background.

In the next, Cara was driving, dramatically putting on her sunglasses and turning up the radio. It wasn't my playlist. That had come home with me.

In the next, she was on the side of the road, a Welcome to California sign in the background.

I sat up straighter.

"That's right, guys. I'm finishing the journey alone, but damn it, I'm going to finish it. Fingers crossed my boss isn't on Mesmio. She thinks I'm still stranded in Arizona."

There were several after that with minimal monologue from Cara, just views of Joshua Tree National Park, waterfalls, a cupcake with a dried mango parrot perching in the icing, and the Pacific Ocean.

That was the most recent reel. Cara looked windblown and happy, the early sunrise turning the mountains behind her into black silhouettes.

"This is the first time I've ever seen the Pacific Ocean. The water is so cold, and the waves are so huge—I don't know how anyone swims here. Maybe they just surf." She turned the camera out to catch surfers in wet suits rising and falling on the waves. She looked around. Left and right, the beach stretched out, endless and almost empty.

Cara gave a *wow* face to the camera.

I watched it again, my heart as full with her happiness as it was empty with the knowledge that I should be there with her.

This was our adventure. I had abandoned it and her, not without reason. But still. I ached to be there with her.

Maybe one day, we could salvage our friendship.

But I was still in the process of ending a marriage with someone I couldn't trust. I wasn't eager to jump back into anything more than friendship, certainly not with someone who had already proven that she could lie to my face.

I tried to turn my attention back to the store's books, but the bell over the door rang three times in five minutes, so I abandoned my desk with a sigh and went to see what was happening.

What was happening was that Strings & Things was fuller than I'd ever seen. I noticed something else, too, that I hadn't before. People turned to look at me and smiled and turned back to their friends to whisper.

Oh God. Was I a Mesmio celebrity?

My fears were confirmed later when a young woman came up to me and very enthusiastically told me all the reasons Cara and I were soulmates.

And she wasn't the last that day.

Fortunately, most people who came into the store that day were actually interested in making purchases. Several mentioned that they had seen me play a song online and followed the link for information about Strings & Things but didn't seem to know anything else about Cara and me.

Sure enough, when I had a spare moment to check our Mesmio stats, my song at the rental house near the hot springs had ten times more views than any other, and Cara had, indeed, put in a link to the store's website.

After the store closed that night, Florence and Doug waited for me while I took a look at the register numbers.

"You're right," I confirmed to Florence. "It's the most profitable day in the store's history."

"I knew it," she said. "Can't sneak a chicken past a chicken hawk."

I turned to Doug. "Want to work full-time?"

He did.

I sent them home for the night, and even though I really needed to go home, too, and pack up the house, at least the part of it that was inarguably mine, I balanced my phone on a shelf against some packs of ukulele strings and started recording.

I'd created a new Mesmio for the store. It didn't feel right to post on the one Cara was still using, though I'd probably go through and message some of our followers there in the next few days, inviting them to follow the store, too.

I felt like I had a thousand songs in my head, everything that had been percolating during the trip, everything I'd worried about since.

But I started with the one I sang the night before everything fell apart for me and Cara.

I'd added some lines, changed a few things here and there, and when I watched it, I realized that I hadn't looked at the camera once. I was focused on the guitar in my hands. But the display of electric guitars behind me was gorgeous, so I went ahead and uploaded it.

I didn't want to be a celebrity of any kind, but I wanted to keep running my business. If a video now and then would help that happen, well, Doug was full-time now. It could be his job.

Chapter Thirty-three

In the morning, Cara posted a new reel.

I opened it, and there were the redwoods. They were giant and ancient, rising so high that it seemed to take Cara ages to turn the camera to the tops. The colors were so rich that I could hardly believe they were real. Every angle, every view was breathtaking. I couldn't imagine how much more breathtaking it was in person.

Cara showed the trails, a cluster of ladybugs on a branch, a child napping in the shade of a massive tree trunk, and more people—people in hiking gear, people with expensive cameras—most of them silent because what could they say? There aren't words for beauty like that.

Eventually, Cara turned the camera to herself. She'd found a bench, and her eyes looked teary, but not swollen. She was overwhelmed in this moment, maybe, but she wasn't still spending her days crying.

"You have all been so kind," she said. "You know this trip was a mix of planned and unplanned adventures." She gave a little laugh. "And thank you, most of you, for respecting what I said when Honey went back home. I don't know"—she paused and shook her head—"I don't know if she'll ever watch this. But Honey, I made it. I finished the trip."

She gave a sad little laugh and showed the trees again as she went on, "I made it, and I did it alone, and I'm proud of that. But I also thought a lot about what you said at the Grand Canyon, about being alone not being any kind of victory. That we, people, are made for each other. I don't know if I believed you, really. But now I do. I wouldn't be here without you. And I wouldn't be able to sit here and see this beauty in the same way if you hadn't shown me how. Well, you and Mary Oliver."

She turned the camera back to herself, and she was blushing. "You left one of your books. I'll make sure to get it back to you. I made sure that I wasn't eating Cheetos while reading it, so any orange stains on the pages are yours alone."

I smiled, surprised to feel tears forming in my eyes.

"Honey," she said, "you asked about my aspirations, and I told you that they weren't job-related, but I wouldn't tell you anything more. The truth is that I was embarrassed not to have any aspirations. No ambitions. Career or otherwise. I've spent my whole life doing what my parents wanted, doing what my husband wanted, and that day I walked into your music store and asked you to take this trip with me was the only time in my life when I've made a big decision based on what *I* wanted. Me. No one else. I thought not traveling alone was a failure, but you're right. It wasn't. And from now on, whether I go alone or…or not, I'm going to be figuring out how I want to live my life. I'm going to be asking the question, and even if I don't find the answer, I won't stop asking."

There was a pause, a moment when it was just Cara and me, looking at each other across this distance.

Then she smiled. "Thank you, Honey. I'll be back in town in a week. I…I'm going to take the long way home."

I didn't watch the video again. I sat with my phone in my hands, in a house half full of boxes.

Bridget had never read a single poem, even when I asked her to. It wasn't a comparison, exactly. I wasn't thinking, gee, Cara's a much better person because she'll open a book. But I couldn't help but see that she was reaching out to me in a way that felt more tangible than saying my name on Mesmio. She was reading what I loved, to know me better, the same way she'd listened closely to my playlist, even the songs she decided after that she didn't like. The same way, when I said *Look at this view*, she stopped and looked.

It was lovely, when someone made an effort like that.

I tried to set my thoughts aside long enough to get some packing done before work. I had a couple of hours, but then I had a midmorning tour at an apartment complex nearby. I needed to get moving.

I connected my phone to the living room speakers and, after a moment of hesitation, started our road trip playlist.

I filled box after box with the detritus of my married life. I'd expected to have to think about each object, to make serious decisions about what was Bridget's and what was mine, but it was easy, in the end. These were the knickknacks, the art, the coffee mugs I'd picked out. These were the other things, the ones Bridget had bought or used far more than me. It began to feel like our lives had barely overlapped.

And that made me start thinking about what I wanted my next relationship to be like, whenever that happened. I wanted to buy only things we both loved. I wanted to use everything, every plate and pillow. I didn't want to make those decisions alone anymore.

I thought about Cara's clean house, her porcelain dishes, her extra-fluffy towels. I imagined arguing with her, a thousand fierce and absurd arguments over houseplants and the thermostat and which movie to see. Cara would have an opinion, she wouldn't give in because it was easy or because she didn't care. That was a truth about Cara that felt integral to her: She cared.

I shook the thoughts away and returned to my packing. I filled and duct-taped another box, pushing it next to the others by the front door, where Badger sniffed it suspiciously, then jumped on top and looked at me, waiting for praise for his accomplishment.

I packed half the pots and pans, half the mismatched cups and glasses. I left everything I hated: the slow coffee maker, the ancient vacuum cleaner, the couch, most of what hung on the walls.

And I couldn't help it—I looked for clues that I might've missed. Were there love letters in that shoebox? Condoms in this old purse? I didn't pretend to respect Bridget's privacy. I searched everything, everywhere.

But there was nothing. There was no way I could've guessed that Bridget and Lorenzo had been together for months.

Finally, I took the picture from my bedside table and stared at Bridget and my younger self, so beautiful in our wedding gowns, beaming with joy and love and hope.

I took a special trip to the dumpster and tossed it, and when I heard the glass shatter, I didn't look back.

After Cara had come into the store that first day, asking if I knew, I'd wondered if I *should* have known, if the evidence was everywhere and I'd been too in love or too self-obsessed or just too busy to notice.

But no. Here I was, looking for the evidence, and there was nothing.

So why had Cara come to the store that first time? Why ask if I knew? What difference could it have made to her?

It was one more question that I hadn't thought to ask.

Maybe once Lorenzo was gone, she was looking for someone else to blame. But that wasn't Cara.

What would have been going through her mind? I tried to put myself there, in her place, walking through the door, hearing the little bell ring.

I thought of today's Mesmio reel, about her trying to figure out what her life would be from now on.

She was grieving, full of disbelief that her marriage was over, full of blame, but not toward me. No, if I knew Cara, she already had a target for all that loathing: herself.

She was hoping…she was hoping that I'd known about the affair for months, too. That I'd done everything I could to save my marriage, too. That we could both feel foolish and betrayed and angry together. That by sharing it, maybe we could carry the weight.

Because Cara hated to go it alone.

My eyes closed in pain for her.

It was a guess, all of it, but I had no doubt that if Cara and I ever spoke about it, she would tell me that I was right. Consciously or subconsciously, she'd only been looking for an ally in her pain.

Chapter Thirty-four

I started driving by her apartment on my way to work. It was on the way, I told myself. I didn't stop, just slowed enough to look for a bright orange car, a little worse for wear.

She said she was taking the scenic route, and I checked Mesmio often, but she'd stopped posting. I worried about her. If she was out there on the side of the road somewhere, would another Mildred and Jeffrey turn up to rescue her?

I started going by on my way home, too. She still wasn't back, so every day, I went home and fretted while I packed and drank.

I wanted to reach out to her, everything else be damned. I wanted to touch her over the distance, to hold her hand, to soothe her worries. When had this happened, this obsession with whether she was happy or not? I was happier when I was just obsessed with her lips, but now, I wanted to see those lips so I'd know if they were smiling or frowning, and whether I was the cause.

The worst thing was that I *could* reach her. This wasn't a Victorian romance when all I had were letters and weeks of waiting. I could call her or text her. I could make her a reel. I could get back on a goddamned plane and go get her. I couldn't stop being aware of all the options I was too cowardly to take.

I'd started my own business, gotten married, and survived the failure of my marriage. I did what I wanted to do. I believed in living bravely and taking chances, even, occasionally, stupid and impulsive chances.

But I couldn't call Cara. I got the same paralyzed feeling as when I'd stood in my office a week ago, holding the envelope that would tell me I was getting divorced. I couldn't do it. I was worse than a chicken. I was a rabid javelina who disappeared as soon as her back was turned.

I laughed, snorting wine.

"This is what pathetic looks like," I told Badger. "You may not be familiar with the sight, but you should get used to it."

Cara and I hadn't talked about what our incredible day together meant. There hadn't been much time, but maybe there was another reason. Maybe we hadn't been eager to ask questions neither of us could answer. We were married, both of us ending long relationships, both of us recently heartbroken. It wasn't smart to think about a real relationship, let alone talk about one.

But I didn't have to think about it to know that what I felt for Cara wasn't casual. It wasn't a momentary attraction, a fling of opportunity. God, I wish it had been. That would've been much more convenient.

It wasn't fleeting, but what was it? Or I supposed the right question was, what could it have been? I would've given a lot to find out what we would've become, with time, with freedom, with a return to our normal lives with all the associated pressure.

I thought, for the first time, about Cara in my real life, stopping by my store, coming by my new apartment, helping me find those little things, those porcelain sugar bowls, to make my everyday life a little better, a little nicer, a little sweeter.

God, I missed her.

In between worrying about and missing Cara, I ran a busy, thriving store while trying not to get my hopes up that the change was permanent. I'd been right about Doug's ability to handle Strings & Things's social media presence. Once he had permission, he was posting content on sites I hadn't even heard of.

"What's a Facebook?" I asked, then grinned when his eyes went wide.

"It's like the white pages for college students," Florence contributed seriously. Doug and I just laughed.

I wrote a few songs for our Mesmio page, and our followers grew, but not the same kind that Cara's and my account had. These followers wanted to talk about music and instruments and songwriting, and I found that, whether they were in the comments section or the store, I liked talking to them, and I learned a lot, even switching some of the store's products to ones that were more ethically produced, on a follower's recommendation.

This was what I'd envisioned when I first dreamed about opening a music shop. It was more than a store. It was a place for people to share what they loved.

Cara had teased me about remembering everyone's name, but when I recognized one of the store's followers before they recognized me, I appreciated for the first time that not everyone had that gift. The guy was delighted and came in to make purchases twice that week.

At Doug's recommendation, a few of our regulars stayed after hours and recorded their own songs to post on the store's page, and our views and followers skyrocketed.

I woke up each day in my new apartment overlooking Houston's Discovery Green and acres of trees, feeling in awe of how quickly my life had changed. I remembered the empty store of a few weeks ago, my stress about keeping the doors open and what would happen to Doug and Florence if I had to lay them off, and how lonely I'd been without Bridget, a bone-deep loneliness that I hadn't want to name but that I'd felt every single waking moment.

And Cara had changed all that. Not only had she come along and been a friend to me when I needed one, but because of her, I was now part of a musical community unlike anything I'd known since college.

More and more, I looked forward to saying thank you. More and more, I wanted to sit with her on my balcony and listen to the live music in the park below and tell her how much better my life had been since she'd walked through my door.

Of course, none of my newfound success was going to stop me from stalking my ex-wife's Mesmio for a hint that she was secretly miserable. Maybe I should be more mature. But I wasn't.

I had finished signing our divorce paperwork—while listening to Selena Gomez's "Single Soon"—with one change: I was keeping our dog, and I wanted it in writing.

Bridget had agreed without argument.

There was nothing on her Mesmio about the divorce. I don't know why I expected that there would be. Maybe it was too serious a topic for her brand.

Bridget and Lorenzo had long since returned from their cruise.

Now their videos mostly showed them at different places around Houston and Galveston, walking along the seawall, eating expensive food, trying out new bars.

One day, they were touring Saint Arnold brewery, which was weird because I was pretty sure I'd never seen either of them drink a beer.

But there they were, clinking glasses, smiling with foam mustaches.

"*Sometimes it's not about the adventure,*" Bridget said to the camera, blotting her mouth with a napkin. That soft, happy glow she'd carried for months had only grown brighter. "*It's about seeing the world for the first time through the eyes of someone you love. It's about feeling that one single place isn't big enough for everything you feel.*"

She looked at Lorenzo, who was staring adoringly at her, and I had to notice that he, too, looked more relaxed and happier than I'd ever seen him.

Still ugly, though.

"*You are my adventure,*" she whispered.

I made an elaborate gagging sound as I closed the app, for no one's benefit but my own.

"They are the worst, aren't they?" Cara said.

I dropped my phone on the cash register, and it bounced onto the floor. I bent to get it, my heart pounding.

I hadn't noticed the bell over the door, but it rang so often now that it didn't jolt me the way it had only a few weeks ago.

I stood, knocked my head on the counter, then gave up and just sat down on the floor.

Doug rushed over. "Are you okay?"

"Fine. Would you watch the register for me for a while?"

"Of course," he said, then looked up and saw Cara on the other side of the counter, and his mouth dropped open like a cartoon character's.

Chapter Thirty-five

Cara looked calmer than the last time I'd seen her, sobbing on the couch at our shared vacation house. She wore a dress I hadn't seen before, black with tiny embroidered vines at the waist. Her eyes weren't red and swollen, and she didn't seem to be angry. She was lovely. I wanted to keep staring at her, to take in every detail and remember them all, but I was still sitting on the floor in a busy store.

I stood and dusted myself off, even though I'd vacuumed the carpet myself that morning, and used the moment to take a second look at her expression.

I confess, even after watching her Mesmio reels, that I'd expected her to be pissed off. I would be, if she'd abandoned me in the middle of a road trip to fly home.

Maybe not if she'd had a sick dog. I'm not a monster.

Still, I met her eyes and winced. "I am so sorry."

Cara looked around. We had a lot of eyes on us. "Can we talk somewhere…else?"

I led her back to my office, which had always seemed fine to me, but with Cara in it, there was something lacking. Coziness, maybe? I wanted to offer her something other than a plastic chair that looked like it had come straight out of a middle school classroom, but it was all I had. My own desk chair wasn't much better.

"I'm sorry," we both said instantly, then laughed.

"A good start," Cara said.

I agreed. "How was the rest of your trip?"

Cara spent a few minutes telling me about Muir Woods, Death Valley, Cloudcroft, and stopping to see real dinosaur footprints. But I could tell that wasn't why she was here.

When she'd finished, she handed me a book. Mary Oliver, *New and Selected Poems, Volume One*. Winner of the National Book Award was printed across the top of the cover.

"This is yours. Thank you for…forgetting it." She gave me a half smile.

I opened it and looked at the writing inside, at the almost perfectly circular *O* of Mary Oliver's signature. Then I closed it and pushed it back across the desk to her. "I want you to have it," I told her. It was an impulse decision, but one that I already knew I wouldn't regret. What would Mary Oliver do in this situation, but share something precious with someone she…she cared about very much?

Cara took the book back gently, holding it in her hands.

"I met her once," I said, "when I got the book signed. She was just a normal person."

"I can see that." Cara was nodding slowly. "She said that our work in life is to pay attention, and I…" She paused, shaking her head. "I didn't know how to do that before you." She raised her head and met my eyes. "I could buy things here and there to make my life more comfortable, but I didn't want to look more closely than that. I was afraid of what I'd see. I was afraid of being alone. I was afraid of everything, Honey. Absolutely everything."

She laughed a little at herself, eyes moist. I didn't interrupt. I was grateful for my quiet office. Doug must have passed the word to Florence not to bother us, and the discordant racket of aspiring guitar players barely reached us.

Cara went on, "Then there we were, driving across the country, and so many bad things happened." She shook her head again, then seemed to feel that wasn't enough and shook the book, too. "So many! Nothing catastrophic, but nothing that I could've brushed aside, either. I kept wanting to let it all build up, and you kept letting it all wash over you like it was part of the adventure. Broken elevators, animal attacks, a rainstorm breakdown, a motel that the health department should really shut down, terrible coffee—you could laugh at it and then keep enjoying everything else."

"I'm very good at denial," I tried to joke.

"I think what you're good at is living. Like her."

I was speechless. I was very nearly breathless. No one had ever given me a compliment that mattered more.

"And did you know," Cara went on, "that I didn't get tired of you?"

"What?"

"That whole trip, all the days in the car, I still wanted to be with you at the end of every day. I missed you so much when you left, but I understand why you felt like you had to get away from me. Honestly, I wanted to get away from me at that point, too. And I know I said it, and will probably say it again. I'm sorry. I should've told you about Bridget and Lorenzo the moment I found out. I was selfish, and I've spent ages hating myself for it."

"I don't know that I wouldn't have done the same," I said. "And I'm sorry for just leaving. I should've stayed and communicated like an adult."

Cara grinned. "Adulthood is so overrated."

"Cara, you might not have gotten tired of me, but…"

"But you're tired of me?" Her expression turned sad, but sympathetic.

"No! No, I'm sorry." I laughed a little. "That was a bad place to pause. I was trying to say that when I'm with you, I don't feel lonely. It's a strange feeling. I'd been lonely so long without thinking about it that it took me by surprise to feel connected."

"That must've made my betrayal feel even worse."

I shook my head quickly, then nodded. "Well, yes."

She sniffed a laugh, her eyes glistening.

"But it made my reaction worse, too. You came into the store that first day and changed absolutely everything. And I think I understand what you were looking for, when you came looking for me. It wasn't about blaming me or trying to hurt me or even about getting answers. You came because you didn't want to go through it all alone. You wanted to be with someone who would understand how much you were hurting, and you picked me."

She shook her head. "I didn't want you to be my therapist."

"No," I said, rolling my chair to the side of the desk so I could take her hand. "You wanted me to be your friend. And I'm so glad you did, Cara."

"So am I," she whispered.

Chapter Thirty-six

It would've been easy, at that point, to fade out of each other's lives. We didn't live or work in the same parts of town. We could move on, consider our trip a failed experiment, and pretend not to notice if we ended up in the same grocery store aisle one day.

But I hadn't been lying to Cara. Everything else aside, her friendship meant a lot to me, and I intended to keep it.

So the next morning, I texted Cara to ask if she wanted to come see my new apartment on Sunday. She agreed, only if I would let her help by unpacking some boxes and listening to her sage advice on where to put everything.

"You can't just throw things around willy-nilly and hope you end up creating a comfortable space," she said the moment she arrived. "You have to plan."

"What about nilly-willy? Is that an acceptable alternative?"

She picked up a pillow from the top of a stack of boxes and threw it at me.

Badger yipped in protest, then, duty done, rolled over at Cara's feet in expectation of belly rubs. Cara acquiesced, adding in some baby talk, which made Badger's ears perk up lightning fast.

"Have some dignity," I told him. He lolled his tongue at me.

I had worried that it wouldn't be the same with Cara and me, now that we were back in our regular lives. Maybe we had only liked the vacation versions of each other. Maybe it would turn out that we had nothing in common past a few days on the road and a couple of memorable nights together.

Or maybe not. Maybe all we needed was a little thought, a little effort, and a trip to a gourmet popcorn store.

I'd stocked my new pantry with fourteen kinds. Cara had gone wide-eyed when she found them, immediately insisting that we put some blue kernels in my new air popper.

Cara ate the first popped kernel, disappointingly white, not blue, and made a soft happy sound that was so familiar that it stopped me where I stood in my new kitchen. The last time I'd heard that sound, I'd been kissing her neck at the hot springs, my arms wrapped around her, pressing her against me, skin to skin.

"Water?" I offered with a croak.

Cara and I unloaded most of the kitchen and bathroom boxes. She organized dishes by frequency of use, so I no longer had to stand on tiptoe for coffee cups every morning. She found cabinet space for any appliance I didn't use at least once a week, freeing up my counters. She alphabetized my medicine cabinet and threw out my expired cough syrup.

"You packed expired cough syrup," she said, baffled.

"I kind of threw stuff into boxes without looking too closely."

"Clearly."

When she stopped, it was to shake her head at the ragged state of my towels. "We have to fix this immediately. Let's go shopping."

We went shopping. I followed her through the store, watching each expression on her face.

I'd been convinced that we could make this work. We'd apologized. We'd forgiven each other. I'd bought popcorn. We were friends again.

But seeing Cara rub her soft hands over the towels at the store was a challenge for which I was not prepared. I watched her hands caress the fabric, fingers pressing the slightest divot in the cloth. She slowly smoothed the surface with her palms.

She bit her lip thoughtfully, comparing textures.

I hurried to the next aisle, pretending to study toothbrush holders and steadying my breath. It was perfectly normal to be jealous of towels. Not strange at all. And how great was it to have friends? Friends were great. This was so…great.

Cara found me a few minutes later. She had a stack of towels and matching washcloths in her shopping cart. I wondered if I would ever be able to use them without thinking about her hands.

I pushed away the thought and held up a cactus-shaped toothbrush holder in an unnaturally vibrant shade of green.

She squinted. "Whatever makes you happy, Honey."

"Then I definitely need the matching soap dispenser."

That evening, we took a break from unpacking and sat on the balcony in my former backyard chairs, sipping glasses of iced tea and listening to a blues band playing in the park.

We had talked about doing a short video for our Mesmio followers now that Cara was back, and unusually for us, we planned out what to say ahead of time, commemorating the end of our trip and closing out our Mesmio series.

Now, I pointed the phone camera at Cara. "Look who's home!"

She smiled. "Houston is definitely home. If you haven't gotten around to visiting Honey's store, Strings & Things, you absolutely should. I was there a couple of days ago, and it's a music-lover's paradise."

I turned the camera to capture us both.

"Now, you aren't a musician yourself, are you, Cara?"

"I rocked a mean triangle in middle school, but otherwise, no, Honey."

"So for the other latent musicians, what might *they* find of interest at Strings & Things?"

"Well, Honey, you can always learn something new, buy a gift for a friend, or if nothing else…it's a good place to pick up a guitarist."

It was a scripted joke, and not a particularly good one, but Cara delivered it with a wry smile, and her eyes were on me, not the camera. I'd have to edit out the part where I returned her gaze and was the first to look away.

I got us refills of iced tea and held my own cold glass against my burning cheeks before going back out to the balcony, Badger whining to join us.

The music from the park below had picked up in tempo, and Cara was leaning back in her chair, eyes closed, soaking in the melodies and the last of the sunshine, her smile content. I'd imagined us just like this, relaxing here at the end of a busy day, legs outstretched, her mauve-painted toes inches from mine.

My fourth-floor balcony provided an excellent view of the hundreds of beautiful old oak trees, people flying kites, and children playing in Gateway Fountain.

"Badger is terrified of that fountain," I said.

"It's water shooting up twenty times his height. I think I'd be scared, too. I'd be wondering, why is this bath so aggressive?"

I snorted. Below, one of the kids squealed loud enough to be heard over both the traffic and the blues band.

"How does Badger feel about the balcony?"

I risked a glance, but Cara wasn't looking at me. She had leaned forward to watch the rhythm of the fountains as the water surged and collapsed. It could be hypnotizing.

"I haven't let him out here yet," I admitted. "He would have no trouble wiggling between the bars, and it's a long fall."

"We'll find some balcony netting," Cara said, measuring the distance between the bars with her hand.

"Or I could buy him a collar with really big spikes."

"Yes. Forget about what I said. That is the solution."

I laughed, and she grinned at me, glowing golden in the sunset, the scattered light bringing a shining warmth to her breeze-tousled hair. It wasn't the first sunset I'd spent with Cara, not by a long shot, but this one seemed to touch her more gently. She seemed relaxed, and it was a good look for her. It was one I'd like to see more often.

"Do you think you'll like it?" she asked, her voice low.

I realized I'd been staring and tried to find my ice cubes as fascinating as I found Cara. "Like what?"

"Like living here. After owning your own home, after sharing your space for so many years. Do you think you'll be okay with this?" She gestured back to the apartment that was, thanks to her, mostly unpacked.

I looked toward the apartment, to Badger's face pressed against the glass door, to the balcony and the beautiful view, then to Cara. "I think I do like it. I think I should've made the move a long time ago."

"Making the moves—" Cara stopped herself, as though she'd realized it was, maybe, a joke she shouldn't make.

"What about you?" I asked quickly.

Cara shrugged one shoulder, turning back to look out over the park. "I don't know about me. I think…I think I'm happy, actually. Is that strange? This whole year has been…let's say *turbulent*. Because it's been bad and good, both, but never calm. I think I'm looking forward to some calm."

I nodded slowly, absorbing her words. "Calm sounds incredible."

"Doesn't it? It's iced tea and a blues band and a sunset. It's hard to get more perfect than that."

She grinned, and I saw every wrinkle beside her eyes, the lift of her cheeks, the glimpse of her teeth, all so familiar and so new, and all I wanted in the world was for her to have a hundred thousand calm evenings and a million perfect smiles, and if she wanted me there, too, I'd be there, but more than anything—God, more than *anything*—I wanted her to be able to say *I think I'm happy* every day for the rest of her life.

But I didn't know how to say any of that. So instead, I told her about everything that was new with Strings & Things, about Badger's upcoming vet appointment to get a rabies booster shot, and about how my mother had tried to sign herself and my dad up for an Introductory Weight Lifting for Seniors class and accidentally signed them up for Introductory Wine Tasting.

"Oh no," Cara said.

"Yes, my dad pretended to be upset about the mistake for a whole five minutes. Now he uses words like *bouquet* and *herbaceous* and *velvety* every time we talk. He's become so obnoxious that my mother threatened to cancel their tuition payment if he doesn't cut it out."

Cara laughed. "At least you know that they won't be pairing rosé with steak the next time you're there for dinner."

"Yeah." I set down my glass, thinking. "Yeah. You should come, too."

"What?"

"To dinner. My parents have heard so much about you, and they watched all our reels."

Cara seemed to blush a little at that, as though making our videos was something completely different from people actually watching them. It was, I supposed. Even I sometimes managed to forget our brush with internet fame.

"I would like that," she said, grinning that grin again, shining in the sunset glow.

I watched her, hearing myself add, "But only if the wine is good."

"Right," she said, meeting my eyes. "Only if the wine is good."

Chapter Thirty-seven

The sky was almost dark when Cara said she should be getting home. I didn't argue, not because I didn't want to, but because I didn't know how to ask her to stay without sounding needy. I'd told her I was okay in my new apartment alone, and I was. I didn't need her to stay and keep me company. I had Badger, who had wiggled himself halfway under a pile of throw pillows and fallen asleep.

When Cara left, I stood at the door, wondering at the empty, aching sensation that started in my chest and radiated outward. It was so unexpected that it took me a minute to identify the feeling.

I missed her. That was all. I just missed her.

I missed her smile and her criticism of my towels and her newfound enjoyment of every experience. I missed the sound of her voice and the way she rolled her eyes at my jokes. I missed every minute we'd had and every minute we should've had and every minute we could still, maybe, have together.

I kept thinking that we could be, that we *should* be friends.

I'd walked out on her, accused and abandoned her. She said she'd forgiven me. She said we could be friends.

That should be enough, shouldn't it? To be friends with Cara Espinoza, I'd be the luckiest person in the world.

I was attracted to her, of course, but I could manage that, shove it down deep and bury it like healthy people probably don't do. But I thought that was an option. I thought I would need time to wrap my mind around everything that had happened and to find my imaginary happy place where I'd accepted the past and was ready to move on.

I'd thought it would be good for me to focus on my business and this new stage in my life before I considered a real relationship.

I'd thought that she would be okay, and I was right. She was fine. She was happy.

But I'd also thought the same about me, that my life would be okay, with or without her.

And I was wrong.

The thought was staggering.

I was wrong.

I'd been so wrong. I'd misunderstood my own heart so completely that I was still standing at my own apartment door, my hands clenched, my heart pounding, my eyes filling with tears.

Would she even want me? Could I take the risk and ask her, or would it be better not to even try?

I put my hands against the door, then my forehead.

And I remembered her at White Sands, running past me, laughing, on her way back up to the top. I remembered her making ridiculous poses with alien mannequins, walking in awe through the cave dwellings, sitting as close to the edge of the Grand Canyon as she dared.

I remembered her at the hot springs, oh how I remembered her there, rivulets of water running down her skin, and the way she'd stepped toward me in the dark and kissed me: the most beautiful woman, the most romantic place, the most sensuous kiss of my life.

My Cara. I had fallen in love with her so deeply, so completely, that I might never find my way out again.

And now that I knew I loved her, the risk of saying the wrong thing seemed so much worse than staying silent. I had to tell her, and I had to do it before the fear caught up to me.

I took another deep breath.

And I opened the door.

Chapter Thirty-eight

Cara stood in the hallway outside my apartment, her face flushed.

I smashed right into her, nose to nose, boob to boob.

"Ow," she said, putting her hand to her face.

"Oh my God, I'm so sorry," I said, reaching out as though I was going to pat her boobs apologetically. She swatted me away, laughing.

"Were you—" she asked.

I asked, "Why—?"

We both stopped, touching our own noses, and laughed.

"Are you okay?" I asked.

Her hand fell away from her face as she tried to stop giggling. "I'm okay. Are you okay?"

"Yes," I said, taking a step closer to her, looking at her beautiful hair, her lovely face, allowing myself to look and be caught looking.

"Come back inside," I whispered. "Please." I didn't want to get my hopes up, but she was still here with me. She hadn't left earlier, and she wasn't leaving now. I needed to know why before my own words spilled out and trampled hers.

Her smile faded. She blinked quickly, her eyes wet.

"No," she whispered back, but she took my hand. "Not until I tell you. If I move from this spot without telling you, I know I'll lose my courage, and I have to…I have to say it."

I nodded, scared to speak. She looked so serious that I had no doubts about what she was about to tell me. She'd say it was too hard to be friends. She'd say that she tried, but it wouldn't work. She'd say that all her friends and family thought it was weird that she'd already spent so much time with her soon-to-be ex-husband's new girlfriend's soon-to-be ex-wife.

She took a deep breath and looked into my eyes.

"I love you," Cara said.

In an instant, my eyes were overflowing with tears, and I didn't try to stop them from falling.

Cara continued, "I'm pretty sure I started falling in love with you the moment you came to my door to apologize for yelling at me in your store." She gave a little laugh, and I stood there, in awe of the sound.

"It was the pastries," I whispered through the tightness in my throat. "No one can resist them."

"It wasn't the pastries, Honey." She squeezed my hand. "It was you. It just took me a little while to realize that the remarkably kind and wise woman sitting beside me was more than just my convenient traveling companion. I've never met anyone I admired more, and that was just the beginning. I love every beautiful and terrifying and ridiculous moment of our time together. I love every conversation, every argument, every one of your awful jokes. I love how much better both boredom and excitement are when you're with me. I love the way the world looks through your eyes and how willing you are to share it with me. And that's all I want. For you to share it with me."

She was openly crying now, too, tears falling faster than she could wipe them away.

I didn't leave her waiting. I pulled her close to me and kissed her, her arms wrapping around me, both of us holding on for dear life. I reached my hands into her hair, curls encircling my fingers. Her lips were better than any daydream, and I had daydreamed. Endlessly.

"I'm sorry," I gasped, stepping back. "I should've asked."

"Don't stop," she breathed, pulling me back to her. "Don't ever stop."

I kept kissing her, walking with her back into my apartment, closing the door, and reaching the hallway without losing contact.

Outside my bedroom door, my lips found just the right place on her neck, and she made that soft, happy sound that she'd made earlier. "Honey," she moaned, and the sound of my name in her breathy voice sent my pulse running but somehow also brought me back to the moment, to her, perfect and gasping against the wall.

I took her hand and kissed it, then pulled her into my room.

I closed the door so Badger wouldn't interrupt us if he woke up.

My new bed frame was still in a box, so Cara sat on my mattress on the floor, and I sat next to her.

Her lips were wet and red and entirely distracting. I closed my eyes for a moment, but even the sound of her breathing was erotic.

"I need to know what you're thinking, Honey."

I almost told her. She would've laughed. Instead, I told her the other things I was thinking, everything I'd been thinking for a while now, and everything I'd just realized. I had felt so bound up, almost mummified, for years, but all that emotion hadn't evaporated. I still had it all. I'd just needed someone to show me what openness looked like. I'd needed someone who'd listen, whether I was making awful jokes or freaking out in an elevator or lamenting my failures over the edge of the Grand Canyon.

"I can't believe you were here, all these years, and I never found you," I whispered to Cara. "I just didn't see, until everything else in my life fell apart. And there you were, rescuing me, and you didn't even know it."

She smiled, and my heart felt full and lighter than air.

"I love you, Cara. I love you so much that I bought a popcorn popper before I bought silverware. I love your meticulous vacation planning, and I love every detour, so long as I'm with you. I love how outrageously sexy you are in red lipstick and with bare lips and first thing in the morning and when you're exhausted because we stayed up too late. I love how you were brave enough to come into my store that day, brave enough to keep going on our trip after I left, and brave enough to come back tonight. I'm in love with you. If you want to know what I'm thinking, that's it. I'm in love with you, and I want to spend every day being in love with you, for as long as you'll have me."

When she kissed me, I felt all my words echoed back to me. I didn't need to hear her say *I love you* again. I could tell. I could feel it in the warm tears on her face and the way she pressed her whole body as tightly against mine as she could.

But I also knew that I *would* hear them, that Cara wouldn't let a day go by without telling me because that's how Cara loved: meticulously and bravely and with her whole outrageously sexy self.

CHAPTER THIRTY-NINE

Cara and I didn't get out of bed until she had to go back to work on Monday morning, and even then, there were few things in my life that had ever been as difficult as letting her stand up and leave the room. It was awful. Entirely too far away from me.

I listened to her turn on the shower and called out, "I can help."

She poked her head around the door, grinning, her hair a gorgeous, tousled mess. "You would be a hindrance, and you know it."

"Oh, you've never been as soapy as I can make you."

"That's the cleanest dirty talk I've ever heard."

I laughed and lay back, grateful for these few extra minutes that Cara could spend here instead of driving home to change clothes. All because I'd accidentally packed one of her dresses in my luggage when I left the vacation house to fly home. It was clean and hanging in my closet, and a few minutes later, Cara was out of the shower. I watched her towel-dry her skin and step into the dress, fastening buttons and smoothing her hands down the front.

"I've never been so jealous of cotton," I told her, then remembered watching her touch the towels in the store and felt an extra hint of warmth in my cheeks.

She kissed me, then went to brush her wet hair. "Are you going to work today?"

"Yes, but I can sleep another hour."

"Ah, the rock star life. I can stop by the store after school, if you want."

"Yes, please. Hey, Cara?"

She turned to me, brush in hand.

"Maybe you should keep a few more outfits here, just in case."

She grinned. "Well, if you think it's a good idea…"

I stood up from my floor mattress and went to her, putting my hands in her wet hair and kissing her clean skin and slipping my hand underneath the strap of her soft dress, caressing her shoulder, her collarbone, the side of her breast.

My teeth teased her earlobe, and somehow, her back was against my bedroom wall, my body pressed against hers. Just the feel of her shape made me breathless. I nibbled down her neck, pushing her other shoulder strap aside.

She made my favorite sound, gasping and unthinking, only existing and feeling and luxuriating in this moment.

The dress caught at her hips, and my fingers slid between the fabric and her skin, loosening buttons slowly. I left it where it fell, lowering my head to kiss the outline of her bra, until she tore it off in frustration.

I kissed the space beside each nipple delicately until she growled and gripped my hair, forcing my mouth where she wanted it. I laughed, then made my tongue soft and caressed her nipples until her body shook.

I ran my hands over her soft skin, trailing my fingers under the waistband of her…wait—

"Did you steal my panties?"

Cara's eyes were dark, her breath trembling. "You want to discuss this now?"

"Yes. I'm about to steal them back."

She laughed, pulling my mouth up to kiss me while I took what was mine.

I didn't break the kiss when she was free of clothes. My hands wandered down over every curve, brushing ever so gently against her stomach, her hips, the insides of her thighs with infinite gentleness, feeling her hot skin with the soft pads of my fingers, patiently exploring her textures.

She moaned against my mouth. "I'm going to be so late for work."

"I can stop," I whispered, moving my fingers infinitesimally. "I can help you get dressed. We can wait until tonight or tomorrow or the weekend…if that's what you want."

Cara kissed me hard, pressing herself against my fingers, then pulled back to look into my eyes. She was breathing heavily, her hair mussed, her lips swollen, her eyes full of passion and happiness and love.

"I think we both know what I want," she said.

"Right," I said. "I'll go warm up the popcorn popper."

She laughed and pulled me close.

EPILOGUE

Two years later

"Disgusting," I said, holding my phone up for Cara.

She looked up from her favorite spot on the soft, squishy couch in our apartment and said, "Ew."

Bridget's Mesmio reels showed her and Lorenzo kissing sloppily at the altar of a wedding chapel. Even the priest looked grossed out. I didn't wait until it started over. I closed out of the app and left my phone on the counter.

I picked up the long, thin envelope I'd hidden behind the juicer we bought last summer and never used. I was so excited I was afraid that I would crinkle the paper. I set it down, then picked it up again. I'd been waiting until Saturday because Cara would want to start making plans, and it wasn't fair to send her to work distracted. But the three-day wait had been excruciating.

From where I stood, I could see into our bedroom. Cara had a picture on her bedside table of the day I'd met her mom and had eaten the best Cajun food of my life. I had a picture on my side of us together at White Sands, me laughing with my mouth wide open, her rolling her eyes at me, neither of us realizing how much we would feel for the other. Not yet.

Cara and I never found out whether Bridget and Lorenzo ever saw our adventure online, though everyone else in our life certainly did. And it had accomplished what we'd intended, sort of. Everyone *had* stopped worrying about our divorces and whether we were devastated and miserable and alone. We cleared that up for them, at least.

In the years that followed, we talked about unfollowing Bridget and Lorenzo, but in a way, it was nice to check now and then, mostly to make sure they weren't having more fun than us, but also because we could acknowledge that they had been important people in our lives. They hadn't realized the gifts they were giving us at the time, but now, I wouldn't give up my divorce papers in exchange for every music store in the world.

I realized I was still holding the long, thin envelope and grinning ridiculously.

"I thought you were researching our summer trip, not hanging out on Mesmio," Cara said, grading the stack of papers on her lap that Badger and Cara's new dog, Cake, an utter cotton ball of a mutt, were trying their best to eat.

"I have been," I assured her.

"Come across any fun ideas?"

"Hmm," I said, sitting down next to her on the couch. "Something like this?"

Jittery with anticipation, I handed her the long, thin envelope.

She went utterly still.

"Open it," I said, lifting Badger and Cake into my lap so they didn't attack the envelope. They shared a deep distrust of mail.

"I'm scared."

"But aren't you also intrigued?"

"Intrigued?" Cara looked at the envelope. "You didn't buy something weird, did you?"

"Only one way to find out."

I was so excited that I hugged the dogs tight until they wiggled free, leaving black fur on one side of my shirt and white fur on the other.

Cara opened the envelope and pulled out two plane tickets, skimming them for information.

"Barbados," she breathed. "How?"

"Travel points, a coupon for a very budget resort, and Doug's promise that he and Florence and the new part-timer we're hiring won't burn the place down while we're gone. Lane will house-sit, water the plants, and check the mail. And my parents will take care of the dogs. Are you excited?"

She looked at me, then put the tickets on the coffee table.

"I think," she said, moving toward me on the couch, "I think the word is *intrigued.*"

And she kissed me.

About the Author

Margo Glynn lives in Houston, Texas, with her family. She is a librarian and amateur gardener, and she is always up for a road trip.

Books Available From Bold Strokes Books

Anywhere with You by Margo Glynn. On a road trip through the Great American Southwest, two friends discover nature, hope, and each other. (978-1-63679-907-0)

Burning Bridges by Lesley Davis. Can Clancy and Jude crack the case of eight missing women—and the secrets of their own hearts? (978-1-63679-872-1)

Dreams Entangled by Sophia Kell Hagin. Amid self-doubt, secrets, a pandemic, fear of attack and attempted murder, Pirin and Gracie's attraction turns to love, and their lives will never be the same. (978-1-63679-892-9)

Echoes of Love by Catherine Lane. As Hazel's and Jo's paths intertwine, they're swept up in a whirlwind of long-buried secrets, sizzling chemistry, and memories that won't be denied. (978-1-63679-835-6)

The Fame Game by Ronica Black. Wild child Hollywood actress Luna Kirkman begins dating Hollywood's leading man, only to fall for his straitlaced sister instead. (978-1-63679-858-5)

Moonlight Obsession by Sheri Lewis Wohl. All it takes to stop a clever killer is moonlight, love, and a silver bullet. (978-1-63679-831-8)

My Boyfriend's Wife by Joy Argento. Amid betrayal and heartbreak, can two women discover a love that could heal their pasts and rewrite their futures? (978-1-63679-866-0)

Tapout by Nicole Disney. A struggling MMA fighter finds her edge in an underground ring, but as she falls for the magnetic and ambitious promoter behind the matches, their dangerous world threatens to destroy everything they've fought to rebuild. (978-1-63679-924-7)

An Extraordinary Passion by Kit Meredith. An autistic podcaster must decide whether to take a chance on her polyamorous guest and indulge their shared passion, despite her history. (978-1-63679-679-6)

Heart's Appraisal by Jo Hemmingwood. Andy and Hazel can't deny their attraction, but they'll never agree on the place they call home. (978-1-63679-856-1)

That's Amore by Georgia Beers. The romantic city of Rome should inspire Lily's passion for writing, if she can look away from Marina Troiani, her witty, smart, and unassumingly beautiful Italian tour guide. (978-1-63679-841-7)

Through Sky and Stars by Tessa Croft. Can Val and Nicole's love cross space and time to change the fate of humanity? (978-1-63679-862-2)

Uncomplicate It by Kel McCord. When an office attraction threatens her career, Hollis Reed's carefully laid plans demand revision. (978-1-63679-864-6)

The Unexpected Heiress by Cassidy Crane. When a cynical opportunist meets a shy but spirited heiress, the last thing she plans is for her heart to get involved. (978-1-63679-833-2)

Vanguard by Gun Brooke. Beth Wild, Subterranean freedom fighter, is in the crosshairs when she fights for her people and risks her heart for loving the exacting Celestial dissident leader, LaSierra Delmonte. (978-1-63679-818-9)

Wild Night Rising by Barbara Ann Wright. Riding Harleys instead of horses, the Wild Hunt of myth is once again unleashed upon the world. Their ousted leader and a fey cop must join forces to rein in the ride of terror. (978-1-63679-749-6